SNIPPETS AND SPIELS

A COLLECTION OF SHORT STORIES

MIKAH RENEE

For the friends and family that made all of this possible:
I love you.

Contents

ANYONE BUT ME

Clinks of cups. Deep blasts of music. Colors flashing in and out.

People on the ground, laughing hysterically. The sharp stench of alcohol.

Nutty foods littering the floor.

The world fading, darkening, lightening.

A flash. A smile.

No, a headache.

I came to groggily, pressing my hand to my head. I remembered it in waves, flashes of lights and sound from late Saturday night. I couldn't recall the time I made it home last night, but I did remember *how* I got home. Climbing drunkenly through the window to my room, quietly but noisily slipping into bed, doing my best to avoid my policeman father. I couldn't even wash out the sickening alcoholic stench until the morning. I did that early Sunday morning before my parents got up.

As I hobbled out of the shower, I found my dad hunched over the dining room table, his hands gliding over his laptop. Concern was drawn on his brow. Something was wrong.

"Are you working on a Sunday?" I asked him. He looked up.

"I am when stupid kids decide to get drunk late Saturday night," he sneered, shaking his head.

I froze. That couldn't have been *my* party, could it? He turned his attention back to the computer, unaware of my change in posture. The headache I remembered from last night suddenly returned, splitting my skull with pain. I tried to shake it off.

I didn't want to ask. "What happened?"

He sighed, waving me over and patting a chair, telling me to sit. I did. "It's some kid in your class - Becca Craft, I think. She and her boyfriend were apparently coming home from this massive party just down the block and their alcohol levels were skyrocketing. Kid couldn't see straight and he drove his girlfriend into a tree. He's facing charges and she's in intensive care. Could've killed her."

That definitely was my party.

Becca Craft, I certainly remembered her. She couldn't stop touching the alcohol, nor throwing it on everyone around her. Her boyfriend, Sean, had a similar issue, except instead of getting rid of it, he'd down it in one go and move to another can. I was honestly surprised Becca, though drunk as could be, even let Sean touch the wheel. He was bound to hurt *someone*.

"That's . . ." I stalled, checking my voice so it didn't waver too much, "awful."

Dad eyed me. He was trained to watch for any body language that contradicts a voice, and I wasn't trained well in avoiding it. I was awful at lying, and I knew for a fact that I hadn't gotten any better. He dismissed it, though, and dropped his eyes back to his laptop. My heart raced.

Too close.

"The charges on this kid, Sean something-or-'nother, are alcohol charges. You should have seen the levels he hit. He could've killed himself if he'd gotten much higher." Dad laughed, but it was dark. Angry. "His girlfriend wasn't far behind him."

I leaned back in my chair, breathing slowly. I could feel my heart in furious detail. It wanted to jump out of my chest. He'd *kill* me if he knew I was there, drinking with Becca and Sean, dousing myself in alcohol and hypnotic lights. I'd be dead in an instant.

Anxiety crept up my neck as he continued on. "It's been only eight hours since the crash, and the whole town knows about it. Do you have any idea how many calls I've gotten this morning? From parents, from your principal, from the station and the hospital and the bystanders from that night? It's driving me insane. People are pressing charges left and right, but they don't even know who they're charging. The party was a raving mystery."

Pressing charges left and right? That didn't sound good at all.

"So what are you doing about it?"

He ran one hand through his hair. "Getting this problem as far away from me as possible. I didn't wanna deal with this on a *Sunday*. The boy had his phone with him and the drunken idiot couldn't stop taking pictures. Or videos. We saw a few of the recent ones but he won't open his phone for us to see the rest of who was there. *Then* charges can be pressed and *then* this problem will be someone else's. I just need his phone open and I'm home free."

A flash. A smile. A shaggy haired boy with his arm outstretched, swinging his phone around for me to see the picture. *Me. Sean. The party.*

I was so gonna pass out. I was in those photos. In those videos. In that stupid, alcohol-reeking boy's phone.

I was gonna have charges pressed. My father, my beloved, proud father, would no longer have a child to boast. My name would be stripped of all good once those pictures were released. I was a good kid in his eyes, a star pupil and a glorious child.

That phone was about to ruin every praise I had ever earned.

My mind began spiraling, telling myself fake truth after real lie. The party was entirely an experiment. *Except it wasn't.* I only went because of peer pressure. *Except I didn't.* I never even wanted to be there. *None of that is true.*

I couldn't even lie to myself. I wouldn't get through this. I had to do something.

"Good luck," I said, unable to control the shake in my voice. On wobbly legs, I booked it to my room. I caught the wary glance my father sent me as I ducked out of the room, and with a start, I realized I might have just given myself away regardless.

Wonderful.

The headache came again, harder this time. Hangover or anxiety, it was killing me.

Something needed to be done. I could *not* let my dad see me on Sean's phone. That night, though I remembered it only in scenes, was a risky night, and I had done things then that could get me in a lot of trouble. Legal or illegal. No doubt the drunken buffoon had also gotten every single chaotic thing I'd done, and I was about to be busted big time.

But what could I possibly do?

My head got worse as my heart quickened. I couldn't really see straight, couldn't really breathe well. I should've known that getting into parties would steal someone's attention. My father was a cop! I'd get the worst of them all for that.

My mind whirred. I couldn't turn back time. I couldn't erase those pictures either, they were there regardless. But I could do other things, things that lifted my blame and laid them on someone else. After all, it was Sean and Becca who got the rest of us in trouble. I wasn't that careless. I climbed through my window, I kept quiet.

It absolutely was not my fault that the party - that I - had been caught.

Why should I take the fall?

Yeah, blame it on someone else. I heard of the party through Alyssa. *One person.* I carpooled with Garret and Winnie. *Three people.* Sean and Becca convinced me to drink. *Five people.* It was Theo's party. *Six people.*

Eight people. Ten people. Thirteen people.

The list grew and grew as one thought bloomed in my head.
Anyone but me.
Absolutely *anyone* but me.

HER COIN

Cameron choked on a strangled gasp, clutching his stomach as he tried to push himself to his feet. He could and couldn't feel *everything*. Everything hurt, but it hurt so painstakingly bad that he couldn't feel it. Raw black bruises stretched up his midsection, sometimes so dark they had been split open into gaping wounds, red blood soaking his shirt. His vision went in and out, in and out, focus to fuzzy.

But he was *awake*. He had to move.

Cameron coughed, spitting blood from his mouth, and winced as the pain splintered through his body. With a grunt, he forced himself up and into the wall, leaning on it to stabilize himself. In the short moment he had when his vision was back in focus, he looked around.

An alleyway. A puddle of his own blood. Two batons.

He was jumped. Left for dead.

His brows furrowed as he tried to remember. Unfocused and dazed, he lost traction against the wall and slid down. He landed with a *thump* back on the cold street. A line of blood was smeared on the wall where he fell, pointing to his barely conscious body.

With what was left of his strength, Cameron reached into his torn coat pocket and fished out a coin, turning it in his hand. It was still here. Still his.

He collapsed as the memories of his beating flooded back into place.

~

Flip. Flip.

Cameron tossed the coin in his hand as he strolled down the streets back home, focused more on the *fwip* of the coin than the sound of his steps. The wind was furious, ruffling his muted black hair and pulling against the edges of his coat. He flipped the coin up again, bring it back down over the top of his hand.

Tails.

The air shifted. Cameron looked up, flipping the coin back into the palm of his hand. The night loomed overhead, a blanket of black, and cast shadows into the nearby alleys. His eyes trailed down the closest one to him, clutching the coin closer to his skin.

There was a glint, a shine in the darkness of the alley.

Something was there.

Then- "Oouph," Cameron coughed as a figure ran into him and kneed him clean in the stomach. The coin spun out of his hand on impact. He collapsed, clutching his midsection, scrambling for his lost coin.

The figure appeared over him again with a cold-hearted glare. Before Cameron could retaliate, the stranger's foot came heavy over his cheek, kicking his head sideways. He groaned and rolled over as he fought the sting of the blow.

"W-Who-?" Cameron mumbled, feeling his mouth with his tongue. All his teeth were still present, luckily.

A baton appeared in the figure's hand. "A friend of a friend."

"Some friend," Cameron spat as he spun up to his feet. Pain

vibrated through his body in tiny little jabs, sparking and fleeting, growing and growing. "Care to elaborate?"

"No," a new voice said. Cameron swung around just in time to meet the swing of another baton, courtesy of a new figure. "He doesn't."

Cameron coughed and leveled himself on the ground with stiff arms. "Please," he groaned. "I don't know what you want."

His attackers circled him slowly. Their eyes moved up and down, left and right, scanning his form. The new one kicked up under him and dropped him to the ground, pinning his body down with his own body weight. Cameron choked on his own spit as he tried to shove off the weight.

"I know you have it somewhere," the attacker hissed, digging his hands into Cameron's pockets. "You have to."

"He may not have it, man. You sure you got the right guy?" The other waited above, letting the search follow through.

Cameron coughed when the attacker shoved him into the ground as he concluded his search empty-handed. "I'm certain." Cameron rolled onto his side. "Where is it?" The baton cracked into Cameron's exposed side. He shrieked, scrambling for air. His lungs fought valiantly, but it did little good.

"I don't know what 'it' is," Cameron moaned.

"The *coin*," the figure snapped, cracking the baton over his side again. The other kicked Cameron in his stomach, turning him face-up. Blood sprayed out of his mouth as he let out a weak cough.

Cameron's breathing was labored, and his insides were churning with prickles of pain. His eyes hurt, bruised and black, and his midsection was torn with blood. Even though he had little left to give, his gaze caught on the glint of his lost coin, blood-splattered but untouched. His only heirloom, his one care in the world, and his late wife's pride and joy. A rarity worth millions, somehow, but something he could never part with.

He remembered when his wife found it, when she tossed it in her hands and discovered the inscription on it - a coin so old and so rare that it could only be destiny that she found it. Cameron felt tears grow in his eyes. They had decided to keep it, together, instead of sell it for a better life because they claimed they'd make their better life together.

That coin was their secret. Was her memory. Was his everything.

He rolled to the coin, scooping it silently in his pocket. Fighting to stay awake, he whispered into the night. "I don't know."

The baton came down again over his head, and the world disappeared into black.

Cameron's thumb caressed the coin as rain began to pour. Little droplets at first, nothing more than a drip here and there, and then the full force hammered onto him. He smiled, though, holding the coin tight. They never found it. He never lost it.

And he'd see his wife again.

With a relieved and hopeful sigh, Cameron closed his eyes and let the rain take him home.

To New Beginnings

I slammed my fridge door closed, rattling the shelves inside. This was *not happening*. He was *not coming to my apartment*. I was *not about to get a ride to work from him*.

None of it was happening.

I drilled the tips of my fingers into my temples and bowed over my kitchen countertop. They were crusted with a thin layer of dust as I wasn't sure I even knew how to hold a pot correctly, but they were a good use of space. Cups and bowls and plates and - were those batteries? - were scattered haphazardly across the faux marble. I was pretty sure there were a couple of old, ugly stains along the edge of the not-so-pristine counter as well.

Regrettably, the rest of my apartment was no different.

And he was coming *here* to pick me up.

I ripped my hands off my head and hurried to tidy up my belongings, though I knew it was hopeless. My best bet was to just keep him from setting foot in this whole blasted building.

But I didn't have his number.

I couldn't tell him to stay where he was.

The only reason I was in this mess was because of my coworker, who was too sick to drive me in to work today and instead reached out to *him*. The one person I told her *not* to reach out to. He was so hard to get along with, but every time I thought of him . . .

I shook my head, cramming whatever feelings that just surfaced back into their little hole. He was hard to get along with. That was it. There was certainly, most definitely no underlying reason for me needing to clean my entire *being* before he made it here. Absolutely nothing having to do with some particularly unwelcome feelings.

My soul practically left my body when two sharp knocks sounded from the front door.

"Adrianne? I'm late enough - are you ready?" I groaned. I ran my fingers through my hair, a wave of messy blonde curls, and snatched my coat and purse. I paused at the door, waiting.

Did I really want to do this?

The door flew open. "Sorry for being such an inconvenience, Sawyer."

I tried to roll my eyes, but it looked more like my eyes were about to fall out of my head. He was sickeningly pretty. He wasn't much taller than me, but his lean build made him seem so much more imposing. Piercing blue eyes and dirty blonde hair were his defining features, so sharp and eye-catching that it was hard to look at anything else. He crossed his arms and sighed, stepping behind me to close my door as I walked out.

"Have everything?" I noticed the way his eyes caught on the inside of my apartment as he shut the door. Sawyer turned to me, one eyebrow raised.

I glanced in my purse momentarily, checking everything off in a mental list. Avoiding eye contact. "I think so."

He straightened the bottom of his own coat and nodded to the side. "Let's go, then."

I wrapped my arms around my stomach as I followed him out to his car. He wasn't really known for allowing others to carpool with him, so I wasn't entirely certain as to why I had even made it into this situation. Sawyer was typically uptight, known more to keep to himself and tune out the rest of the world than actually allow other people near him. He worked efficiently, but it seemed to be the *only* thing he cared about.

In other words, he was known for stomping all over other people's feelings.

My eyes widened as Sawyer made his way to the passenger side door. Something dropped in my stomach when he opened the door and nodded, his hand lingering on the handle. "Get in," he said.

I did. He closed the door and, just as quick, appeared beside me in the driver's seat.

What just happened?

"Buckle," he said blankly, not even looking at me as he said it. The seatbelt clicked into place. "I'm not about to get in trouble for you forgetting a seatbelt."

I just barely stifled a sneer. "If you had given me like two more seconds, the buckle would've been on *without* you yelling at me."

The side eye he gave me made me want to rip my hair out.

He put the car into drive, staring tight-lipped out of the windshield. The car was deathly silent. I turned my gaze out the passenger window to keep my eyes away from him. None of this was supposed to happen. I wasn't supposed to be here. It was easier to just pretend that I wasn't.

But somehow even *I* couldn't hold true to that.

"Why are you driving me to work?" I asked him as I turned to him. He didn't look at me. "You've never made an effort to be nice to me before. Why now?"

Sawyer blinked. "I can take you back home if you'd rather not ride with me."

"You didn't answer my question, Sawyer."

A muscle in his jaw twitched. "I was asked if I could drive you since your car is out of commission. I can be a decent person every so often."

I scoffed. "Fat chance." But then my mind skipped to him holding the door open, a patience and hopefulness in his eyes that I had never once seen before, and my voice died out. Something still didn't add up, but I wasn't sure I could think of it if I tried. I sighed and shook my head.

He grunted, squinting his eyes shut for a moment. His watch didn't come off of the road, though. "I was looking for a window, Adrianne." Some look of pain flashed across his brow, and I sucked down a much needed breath. "Is that what you wanted to hear?"

"A window?"

Finally, *finally*, his eyes turned to me, if only for a moment. "I'm not going to explain what a window is to you. You know what I mean."

"But you've never let other people ride with you before," I told him, bewildered.

"Take that however you like." He turned away as I took in his confession.

"So this window," I started. My hands brushed away some stray lint sitting on my jeans, cuing a spike of nervousness. "Why exactly were you looking for it?"

His hands tightened around the wheel. "Why do you think?"

I frowned. "What do you *want*, Sawyer? Whatever it is that you're not saying, *say it*."

He muttered something under his breath and ripped one hand straight back through his hair, leaving it scattered and messy under his touch. "I can take you to work from now on if you'd like. I can - yeah. If you'd like."

With one hand over my mouth, I smiled. "That was the window you wanted, huh?"

"I'll take it back."

"You can't take it back."

He let out a rough breath. "I don't mean to ignore you at work. Or come off as cold. Part of this was *supposed* to be an apology. The other part was going to be asking you . . . that. Which you didn't answer, by the way. I need an answer."

"I'm thinking," I teased.

"You're not," he said. "You're stalling."

I shrugged. "You're right." Pretending to be lost in thought, I responded, "Okay, I'm sold. Sure."

For the first time in my life, I think I saw him smile. It was foreign on his face, but it didn't look wrong. In fact, it looked like it fit him. Like he had been waiting for a moment to let out that smile from the very beginning. Like a light clicked in him, and I was the one who got to witness it.

I hoped to see it more.

"To new beginnings?" I asked.

His eyes met mine in a quick glance as he said back, "To new beginnings."

JACK(IE) FROST

The campfire crackled. Person after person huddled around each other, using their warmth to ward off the cold of the November night. Hay stuck out of the wires holding the bales together, jabbing everyone who sat on them. Chatter erupted over the snaps of the fire. The night was loud, but in a quiet way. It was welcomed.

"Jackie."

Jackie jumped, snatching her arms back and wrapping them around herself. It was so *cold*. Even the thick black winter coat and double layered pants couldn't keep the sharp prick of winter away.

"Yeah?" She asked.

"What do you think?" The girl speaking to her turned her wide green eyes up to Jackie. She blinked, raising one eyebrow. The girl didn't even look cold.

"I missed your question," Jackie said as she tucked her freezing fingers into her coat.

"Tomorrow," she said, "do you think it will snow?"

"Kendra!" A guy next to her socked her in the shoulder. She

flinched away, slapping at him. "Quit trying to find backup! We're gonna have school tomorrow."

She stuck out her tongue and leaned into his warmth. "Maybe enough hope will keep us from that dreaded place," she said. She turned away from Jackie, forgetting about what she asked, and moved to talk to the guy - AJ - to her other side. Jackie, however, hadn't let the thought slip.

"I think it will," Jackie whispered.

Kendra's head snapped around. The smile on her face glowed brighter than the fire. "You do?"

AJ's jaw tightened. "The chances are so low. There's no way. It's barely even cold tonight."

Jackie shrugged. She hugged herself tighter, nestling further into her coat. *Barely even cold tonight. Sure.* "Where there's a will, there's a way."

Kendra snickered, and she returned the blow that AJ had given her earlier. "*She* knows what's up," she told him. The green eyed girl turned back around, dropping Jackie from her thoughts completely. And so the chatting continued, running deep into the chilly night and leaving Jackie to her sparse conversations with the few around her. The cold bit harder and harder, grappling for her poor fingers and forcing her to press them so deep into her coat it stung. Her cheeks were red and raw, and with eyes half closed, she yearned for the warmth of the fire.

She couldn't feel the warmth tonight, though. It was so close, yet so far. So bright, yet so dull.

Snow would come.

She knew it.

She *felt* it.

It ran through her veins. It was in her bones. The cold was practically speaking to her.

From her left, AJ snickered as he rocked back and forth, Kendra's head limp on his shoulder. She was pressed up against his side with her eyes shut tight, the slight sniffle of a cold-bitten nose sounding every so often. "Not even Jack Frost yet," he said to himself, his breath a cold puff of air. "No snow is coming."

Jackie smiled, pulling her ice-blue hand out of her coat. So, *so* cold.

"I wouldn't say that just yet," she said back to him in a hushed tone.

He glanced up and furrowed his brows as he draped one arm around a sleeping Kendra. Jackie watched.

"There's no signs," he said.

Jackie pressed her hand on the bale underneath her. It was early in the season. Snow shouldn't come for another few weeks at the very least. But the nipping at her ears, her nose, and her fingers meant something was bound to come. And tomorrow, when daylight would overwhelm the land with a sky-high heat that consumed the day - no. That was much too late.

The snow would come very, very soon.

The snow would come *tonight*.

Her hand swirled in circles over the bale, drawing patterns. Snowflakes.

AJ made a low noise in his throat as he kept his eyes on Jackie. "Who are you, again?"

Jackie looked up, leaning back on the hand out of her coat. The other stayed tucked in close, though no warmth would come. Could come, really. She looked up, holding back the smile that itched to come out.

"I go by many names, actually," Jackie murmured into the starless night. The chatter had died down a bit, but the sound of people hadn't. Snores were scattered around the camp. Soft humming filled the air as some silent camp songs were passed about.

Jackie turned her gaze down, back to her free hand. A wave of shock flitted through her as she realized what she'd done. She snatched her hand off of the frosted bale and stuffed it back in her coat.

"What, you have a nickname or something?" AJ asked.

"Many." He nodded forward, urging her to continue. "Jackie."

"So then, what? I'm not sure how many variations of Jackie you can get. Jacklyn? Is that what it's short for?" He readjusted Kendra, still slumped up against him, so that she was in a more comfortable position. Jackie guessed it was so that he was in a more comfortable position too.

Jackie glanced at the frost. She swallowed. "Not quite."

Then she turned to him, not fighting to hide her ice blue eyes. She knew what they looked like when she was in this state - like they had been ripped out of a crystal, so blue it was almost clear, and so bright they almost glowed.

The looked like winter.

Like ice.

Like snow.

Jackie smiled, sighing as she let the cold loose. "The name I go by the most anymore tends to be-" She paused, her vibrant eyes making a quick roundabout as she whispered, just another breeze of the night . . .

"Jack Frost."

Then her eyes turned up, and the snow began to fall.

THE WRONG PICK

My hands twirled the pouch of coins in an experienced manner. I could feel the slick of the lock pick pressed up against my wrist, secured tight with a thief's bracelet. I could always feel it, always aware of where it was and how to use it and when best to make my move. Strolling leisurely through the town's narrow streets, I tucked the pouch away.

I had a big score soon.

There were things I needed to know.

The pick slid down my wrist as I slipped in front of a door, shadowed by the cover of a falling structure nearby. I palmed it, unnoticeably plugging it into the lock and freeing the latch in seconds. With a warning glance at my surroundings, I moved through the unlocked door.

"You're late." The voice was gravelly and irritated as it hissed at me. I turned around to find the green eyes of a redheaded man, full of impatience and fury. I snickered.

"The only thing that matters," I said, dangling the pouch I had tucked away earlier, "is what I will pay."

"That never excused tardiness," the redhead said as he swiveled around. I knew him just barely as an underground messenger - a carrier of information for wandering thieves. He was one not to be messed with, though, as his information usually came from unfortunate circumstances. Word on the street was he went by the Mockingbird.

The Mockingbird moved away from me, nodding his head forward to tell me to follow. I did, warily trailing his footsteps. He stopped before a thick black door, bobbing his head.

"Payment," he said. I flicked the pouch of coins into his hands, and he pressed the door open. The Mockingbird grunted his retorts as I entered the room.

There was a woman.

Her eyes were wide, gleaming against the dull pulsing light above. Her raven black hair was matted and her clothes were tattered as she sat shriveled on the floor, frail and thin. I glanced back at the door again with a grimace. *This* was rather inhumane on the Mockingbird's part.

"Who are you?" I asked her.

"No one - I swear."

"Clearly you're someone if the Mockingbird has you here."

She shook her head, moving away from me. "I'm *no one*."

I raised a brow, pressing my lips flat. "Are you alright?" She was beautiful, in a way, with sharp cheekbones and vibrant eyes, but her sunken skin and drooping eyelids gave away her exhaustion. She didn't look injured, but she didn't look well.

"I'm fine," she said. She frowned, folding her hands over her stomach. "If you really must know, I'm Leah Amelia."

I struggled to keep my emotions in check as she said her name. *Leah Amelia*. "The daughter of Rick Amelia?" She nodded, short and curt, and I stifled a response. I couldn't believe my luck. I couldn't believe what the Mockingbird had found me.

The high and esteemed Rick Amelia was the owner of the largest accessible loot most of the thieves I'd come across had found - a playing card crafted out of a special rare material, worth millions on the market. None of them had the nerve to face the Amelia house though, not without inside information on the job. The *daughter* of the Amelia household was exactly what I needed to ensure the mission was a success.

Leah Amelia was my lockpick.

"Well," she started, giving me a once over. "I might as well know who you are too, right?"

I smiled. "I'm called the Phantom. But you're more than welcome to call me Keith."

I spoke with her for hours. She warmed up to me after a while, her posture noticeably loosening, and information came easier. By the end of our conversation, a promise had been made - my access to her father's house and treasures for her safe return home. It was ingenious, a win-win situation. It was a perfect display of my cunning.

We had taken a carriage to Amelia house, courtesy of a particularly angry Mockingbird. The Amelia girl was hesitant to follow, but after some coaxing, she didn't put up much of a fight. Her trust in a couple of thieves seemed to wear thin, and I didn't blame her for it. Placing a steadying hand on her back, I eased her out of the carriage as we made our stop.

The Amelia house.

It was a stunning place, bathed in riches that poured from every extravagant crevice. It was no surprise that this place held the most desirable loot for the thieves of the area. It was practically asking to be stolen from.

Leah pressed her hands together, twining her fingers tightly in a nervous gesture. "My father won't be home for a while, so this is probably your best time to take whatever it is that you want to take," she whispered.

I followed her to the house, then, letting the Amelia heiress feign control. She had given me everything I needed earlier, and she was about to give me even more. With her opening the door for me, I was just a guest. A friend of the Amelia girl. I was nothing more, certainly not some simple thief looking for a big score. She had given me the layout of the house, the security system in place - *everything.*

I was guaranteed this win.

"Ah," she said as she wiggled the doorknob. "I don't have my keys on me. Could you maybe pick this?"

"Of course," I said with a lazy grin. My hand grazed the door, and just as fast, the door was open.

As it opened, though, I was wafted with a wave of uncertainty. This house . . . it didn't look anything like what Leah had told me earlier. The layout I was previously given was entirely wrong. As I turned to confront her, I found myself being shoved into the open doorway and onto the slick tiled ground.

The Amelia girl was grinning wickedly as she did it.

Then-

Sound - blaring, obnoxious sound. An *alarm.* She had pushed me into a movement detector. I scrambled to my feet, turning to her abruptly. She crossed her arms, tiptoeing into the house.

"You are so *gullible,*" she laughed, ducking around me. As I made my move to abandon the house, her foot came out and slipped in front of mine, knocking me on my face. "Ah ah. I'm getting paid double here. One for a thief," she started. Her eyes glimmered as she flicked her hand into the pocket of her pants and ripped out a card, a silver ace of spades. A duplicate of what *I* had come for. A fake - meant for her to swap with the real one. "And one for a very expensive card."

"You aren't Leah Amelia, are you?" I asked her.

She chuckled. "That's the only thing I wasn't lying about, Phantom. I most certainly am. I just forgot to mention that I have some big scores to make, too." She raised a brow, shrugging. "Whoops."

I sat up and shook my head. This girl was never in trouble with the Mockingbird, I realized. I was just a con - for the both of them.

She tapped my head with the fake card. "Thanks for making this so easy, little thief. You gave me the perfect opportunity to get away with my own robbery. Now I have a little trade to make with some of my daddy's belongings, and I can't have you running off while I'm doing that." Leah crouched in front of me as she cocked her head to the side. "Long story short, Phantom, night night."

Then a white cloth was in her hands, thick with the stench of chemicals, and she pressed it onto my face in one swift motion.

It took mere seconds for me to see darkness. For me to want it.

My last thought as I looked into her cold, conning eyes was-

She was the wrong pick.

SPIRITED

The wind whipped across my face, tearing through my hair and ripping it clean out of the loose bun it was so lightly held together in. My eyes turned to the blue sky, whirling with clouds and gusts of sharp, clean air. The day was awake - stretching its breath of life into the earth and all around. It was blooming.

I took a breath through my nose, inhaling the crisp wind. Scents of spring - of mud and rain and newborn leaves - filled my senses. Colors danced across my vision as I turned my gaze to the ground, where a thicket of dense green trees was nestled, flush against the comfort of the cool blue sky. I smiled, leaning into the whisper of air that blew into my back, and held my watch over the vibrant landscape.

"It's beautiful, is it not?" The voice was light and feathery, practically nonexistent.

I took in the mountains behind, shimmering under the light of the world, and the glow of the lake tucked into the clearing of trees. Beautiful wasn't a word perfect enough to describe it.

"You could call it that," I said.

The voice moved closer, and I didn't dare look for it. I only heard its chuckle as it fell into place beside me. "Few have ever come here," it told me.

I moved to the edge of the rock I stood on, looking out over the stark edge of the cliff. My jacket rustled, fighting against the movement. "Why?"

"Beauty scares men," it whispered. "For what is beautiful is unreachable. Unreachable means unattainable, and therefore their urge is only to destroy what is not theirs." The voice paused, as if in thought. As if contemplating. "Only spirited creatures are allowed to see this light. To see this world. You, my child, are spirited."

"Are you spirited?" I asked it.

Finally, I turned to my companion. She was unreal. Her body was translucent, but her smile shined so bright that she could ward away the shadows if only I asked. Her golden hair rode the waves of wind as if it were water, and her feet, though buried under blades of grass, made no dent in the ground. She met my eyes with a glorious, godly grin.

"I was," she murmured. "Now the Sanctuary has claimed the spirit I once had."

I looked back out to the glittering world beyond, dropping to the ground and dangling my legs off the side of the cliff. The patches of grass tickled my skin, as if painting a message onto my body. Everything about this place was alive and bright, glowing and breathing, but its creatures were few and far between. Songs of birds so colorful they could mesmerize danced through my ears.

"Will it claim mine too, now that I'm here?"

The ghost laughed, dropping her voice in a sigh. "Do you want it to?"

I pondered, rubbing the stone beneath me. "No."

"Then it won't," she reassured me. "It only takes those who submit to it. So long as you are here, you will live until you wish to give your spirit to the Sanctuary." She cocked her head, her thick lashes fluttering. "You could be immortal if you so wish it."

"Immortality is a ruse," I said. "Impossible."

The trees trembled and waved as she said, "Am I possible to you?"

I closed my eyes. "Not by human rules."

"They don't apply here," she agreed. "As your human rules of mortality don't apply here. The Sanctuary is a separate entity from your world, but you are welcome to return home whenever you care to. For the Spirited never lose their spirit, only give it away."

Silence swept across the world, as if in wait for my next response.

"Who are you, then?"

Silence again, cold and dark. My eyes opened.

She was gone.

"Hello?"

I swung in wide circles, surveying the swaying grass, the moss-ridden stone, the singing trees. No hint of the pale ghost lady remained. No steps in the ground, no remnant in the air - just a silent, sleeping clearing of where she once was. I turned back to the view off of the cliff.

"They call me the White Spirit here," the wind whispered. A new song, of sorts, flitted across the barren clearing, now filled with her voice. "I'm more often known as the First Spirit of the Land." She continued singing her answer in the wind. "I lead the spirited through the Sanctuary, or out if they need it. So, new one, tell me. Stay, or leave? I will take you where you choose."

I waited a moment, taking in the glow of the untouched land. A land of immortality, of forever, of nonexistent worries, or the mortal world where I had lived for so long. A choice between a calm forever, or a normal end. A comfortable yet lonely world, or a familiar life.

With one look back out into the trees, the rocks, and the sky, I had made my decision.

"I want to go home."

The White Spirit bristled in agreement, and her soft breeze began pulling me up.

Up and back home, free of the Sanctuary.

Home to mortality.

CLOGGED DRAIN

I couldn't look at him anymore.

Every time I did, things shifted. Things merged. Personalities and people swapped, and I couldn't see the man I once loved.

I just saw the man with crisp blue eyes and flat black hair, with a toned body and a perfect, unwavering grin. I saw the man I kissed in the midst of a relationship, the man I regretted ever letting myself leave.

I saw the fling.

In the past two months, my boyfriend, my brunette army man with a buzz cut and stubble, was never the person I remembered looking at. He wasn't the person I fell in love with every day I saw him. He wasn't the person I had pined over for two years prior to starting a relationship, nor the person who spent the last three taking care of me through thick and thin.

He was the face of a conceited, gorgeous man that I couldn't force out of my mind.

And all I had done was *kiss* him.

"Nessa?"

I heard his voice like a thrum in my ears, quickening my heart. It took me a moment to draw myself back to reality when I realized that the low rumble of his voice had, in fact, not been his.

Xander's brows drew themselves together as he looked at me. I waved him off. "Don't worry about me, Xander," I said, shaking my head.

"I can't help it," he whispered, not taking his eyes off me.

He was a picture perfect boyfriend, a flawless friend, and a great partner, but I averted my eyes. I couldn't look at him. It was awful. I hated myself for this. He didn't deserve any of it.

"Vanessa, please look at me."

Giving my arm a quick squeeze, I looked up to Xander.

Xander was not who I saw. In fact, I wasn't even in my apartment when I looked at him again, I was in a memory. Standing on the beach, feet buried in the sand, watching his eyes sparkle under the moonlight. His lidded gaze followed my jaw, his hand tracing lines in a pattern behind his eyes' trail. Finally, his watch landed on my lips, and mine wasn't far off from his.

We stood there for a moment, listening to each other's breathing, waiting for one of us to call it off. To admit this was wrong. To use common sense.

But we were too close.

My breath was caught in my throat as he moved forward just slightly, his glimmering blue eyes asking permission. Before his face turned my world and heart upside-down, I snapped my eyes shut.

I felt his hand, warm and safe, slide into place just behind my ear.

"Vanessa," he whispered. I could feel his breath on my nose.

My voice wouldn't come.

"Vanessa, I won't do anything you tell me not to. I also won't do anything before you tell me to either." I opened my eyes to look right into his, encapsulated. I couldn't remember Xander anymore, not when looking at him. His eyes sparkled under the moonlight, sucking me into the trance of the fling.

"Then I won't tell you no," I said quietly, moving my gaze to his lips. *I also won't tell you I have someone waiting for me when I get home.*

He was slow and careful, touching his lips to mine at first like a breeze. I let him, molding my own lips to his, only brushing each other's mouths until one of us made a move further.

And he did.

The kiss switched just as fast to passionate, lust-filled and aggressive, sparking a memory of pain and pleasure and stripping away all of my morals. His hand slid up past my jaw and into my hair, clutching fistfuls, pulling me towards him. I let him. I let him I let him I let him. I didn't think in that moment - I couldn't.

In that moment, my senses were full of *him*.

And they've been clogged ever since.

I still have yet to clean the drain.

CORWHISPER

There was a lot wrong with him.

His outrageous fate of living out the rest of his days in an isolated cell was only the start of it.

Why, they'd always ask, was a young redheaded boy locked away for only the roaches to see? He wasn't much to look at. Freckles lined his nose and cheeks, faded from the darkness. His foggy blue eyes hadn't seen natural light in months and had dimmed to a dull gray because of it. He had grown scrawny in the recent months with shaggy, scrappy hair and soot-stained nails. He wasn't anything special.

So why, just *why* was he here?

A scoff gurgled in his throat. Because people would always be afraid of what they didn't understand.

There was this occasional guard who had worked her way up through the ranks that chatted with him every so often. She, somehow, didn't mind what he was. He enjoyed her company, and he hated himself for it. Some days he hoped that she, too, enjoyed his company, enough so to let him go. And yet doing so would tank her good, hard-worked name, and for some reason, he couldn't do that to this guard.

He didn't even know her name. Maybe he'd ask her.

Or maybe, he wouldn't.

Some days she'd turn to him, black eyes only curious, and ask in her lilting voice, "Why is it that you're here, again, boy?"

And he'd retort in little more than a hiss, "Because someone couldn't stand that I'm better."

Then she'd snort.

She'd never tell him if she believed that though. It was the same question every week, and he'd learned to give her the same response. As long as she was consistent, he'd be too. He wasn't going to break any pattern for the pretty, raven-haired lady who lingered outside his cell. He wasn't going to fall for those long lashes or mischievous eyes. He wasn't going to give in.

He hated that he already had.

Conversation only grew with her. She began to smile, to speak, and he'd keep talking just to have more of her there.

"Corwhisper," the guard's voice purred. "Hello."

Corwhisper. Not his name, but his very being. A person who somehow, someway, could speak to the dead. Sometimes he could tell them to do something too, make their body rise from where it once rested and do his bidding. But most of the time, he could only see their wisps, their lives and voices, as they floated around him, begging for someone to talk to. They were lonely without a Corwhisper, and this Corwhisper was lonely without them.

"Crow," he said lightly. He would've called her Raven, a tribute to her pin-straight hair, but she still worked to keep him inside his cell, not out. So crow, the cunning bird that picked around and messed with their targets, sounded better for her. It sounded like the type of bird she was.

"Not talkative today, Liam?"

"It sounds more appropriate if you stick to Corwhisper, Crow.

Try and say it like you hate me too, or else it might give the wrong impression," Liam snapped.

She cocked her head. "It'd sound more like you mean it if you cursed me out, not gave me petty nicknames," Crow said.

"Shall I?" Liam goaded. "Curse you out? Would you like that better?"

Crow shook her head with a chuckle, drawing her ponytail over one shoulder. "It would be funny, to say the very least. As you've never actually cursed anyone out in your life, it seems."

"Incapable." He was raised well. Not even to these cruel people would he stoop so low. He didn't quite have the heart, either. He didn't know why, but he refused to do it.

"Do you know the days anymore, Liam?" Her voice was soft, almost sympathetic.

"Two months, three days. Thursday the fifth of August. It's not going to leave me any time soon." The guard frowned.

"You really are something, Corwhisper."

"I'm only grieving."

Discovering he was a Corwhisper was perhaps the worst moment of his life. He'd never had anyone dead that he needed to talk to. That was, until about four months ago, when a tall man in a wonky hat came to his parents door. He lingered in his room that day, turning a keen ear to his doorway as his parents talked in hushed, strained voices to the man. A collection of gunshots ricocheted through his eardrums. He heard clatters about the house, fight or flight sounds from his sister and parents.

He hid in the closet as soon as the first shot fired. Found a loose board and pushed himself out of the house, somehow, someway.

When the man was gone, he returned. He found his parents dead on the kitchen floor, his sister with a bullet through her forehead in her room. That moment was when he first saw the wisps on their bodies. Their ghostly forms embraced him, happy he was still alive, and in that moment he didn't care that he was seeing the dead. He only cared that his family was still there. That he hadn't lost them quite yet.

Liam had cried that night. He was nineteen, too old to be shedding tears anymore. It was what everyone had told him, at least.

He still wanted to see his family's wisps again, though. He knew, deep in his gut, that it didn't feel right. That it was wrong to see them dead. They had been moved to a graveyard not long after Liam had discovered them. Even still, despite how his insides curled at their wisps, he wanted to find them.

Yet his company was only the roaches and sometimes Crow, if he played his cards right. He instead lived a life of sparing meals, awful living conditions, and rude caretakers.

He didn't even *deserve* his punishment.

"If it makes you feel any better, we *are* searching for your family's murderer. We can't deny the truth in a Corwhisper's words. We will find them," Crow said softly.

Liam ran a hand through his hair and flopped on his cot.

"I only want to hear them again."

Crow adjusted her uniform, tightly fit to her slender body. Liam decided against looking up to her.

"Is it not unnatural talking to your parents and siblings who shouldn't be there?" She turned her back to him. She was the only guard on duty. No one cared to be near the Corwhisper. They didn't find him a threat, not the living. One guard was all that was needed. All that was expected.

And, of course, she was the only guard who truly made him uncomfortable.

Liam sighed. "I feel like it's justified when they're ripped from your life by a gun. My sister was younger than me. She had so much ahead of her. Even if she won't grow as a wisp, she could learn what it's like to grow. If I found her again, that is. But . . ." Liam's voice dropped.

"A wisp," Crow repeated. She tensed. "That's Corwhisper talk for spirit."

"Her spirit is different. It's saved. Her wisp is her remainder, her personality and voice. I could tell you who their killer is, you know. If you let me talk to them. They'd tell me. But you don't care, Crow - that's the reality. They're not actually searching."

Crow turned her head slightly, one careful eye scanning him up and down. "I would search for him myself, but you would be here without anyone to talk to. A shame, really."

"A shame," Liam repeated. "Remind me who between the two of us really wants to talk?"

Crow sucked in a slow breath, but didn't answer.

"Exactly."

A key suddenly appeared in Crow's hand - a small, golden key, the perfect fit for his cell's lock. Liam swallowed, eyes wide.

"Talking to another Corwhisper is an honor, Liam." *Another?* "The last I could not save. She's gone now. But what of the other Worldbenders? If I let you go, Liam, would you fight for them?"

Liam sat up straight on his cot. "I will fight for those who need to be avenged first and *then* I will fight for the living. The dead deserve rest."

"You'd be surprised, Corwhisper. Their rest is permanent no matter how it came to be. You can only fight so far for people who are already gone." She still didn't turn around.

"What about people like me?"

"A lonely Corwhisper without a family?"

"A person who never was given time to heal."

"It's life," Crow whispered. "You'll learn to cope."

Liam scoffed. "You people are doing a lot to help me by locking me in here," he growled.

His cell was intentionally isolated, for good reason too. Prisons like his were rarely taken care of. It wasn't uncommon for captives to die and rot, and if they did - if their cell was near - he could speak to them. He could ask them for help, and while dead, they could give him something to use. They could come to him, live for him, serve him.

So he got a lonely cell. The last Corwhisper's cell, apparently. For the past two months, he lived off of a tattered cot, a small table, a toilet, and a barred door. Not much.

Never much, really.

He'd been taken to a Worldbender prison as the only Corwhisper.

It was so, so lonely.

Click.

The barred door swung open, and Crow watched him with an expressionless stare. Liam didn't move.

"What are you waiting for? *Leave.*" Her black eyes were depthless.

"And what of you?"

"Get knocked down the ranks, maybe fired. But what does that matter to you, Corwhisper? I'm just the guard keeping you locked up."

"It doesn't look very locked up to me," Liam said with a glance at the opened door.

Crow gazed over her shoulder momentarily. "Do you want out or not?"

"I don't want to be on the run. I'm not a criminal."

"Worldbenders don't get out free. It's how this world works."

Crow stepped aside, her dark eyes glinting.

Liam stepped forward without breaking eye contact.

"When you've done your part, come find me," she told him. "The Worldbenders know me. You're welcome to call me Crow for the rest of your life, or you can call me by my true name. They'll know it. Tell them Heather has made her mark."

Liam held her eyes for a moment longer. She didn't break it. After a moment of silence, he ducked away from the cool of her watch and made his escape, all too aware that he'd see her again.

SHARING FIRE

The fire rampages in my head. Swirls and snaps and flares. Whispers and cries, wanders and fades. It consumes my head and thoughts, leaving me stranded.

I open my eyes.

He's there.

The fire is still there, but I see it around him. Like a halo of light, like a tether to my vision, the fire surrounds him. Frames his being. I'm used to it, really. There was always some fire in his heart. It came out in short bursts - when he smiled at the golden sun, when his eyes turned light as he descended deep in thought. But it wasn't until he handed me a piece of that fire, a flame to keep, did I notice how it *consumed* him.

How he was the flame.

My heart strains in my chest at the sight of him. That piece of flame that he gave me - it longs to reunite. His honey golden hair glistens in the morning light. I take him in silently. His breathing steady, he trails one fine-boned hand over his opposite arm, scanning his surroundings. His eyes, a glistening blue so full of flame that they burn brighter than the sun itself, jump to me momentarily. He lets out a smile, a small grin of acknowledgement, and the piece of my fire screams.

I bite down on my teeth.

He handed me the fire not long ago, long enough ago that I still turn away - still disappear - when his burning eyes meet mine. We had known each other for an eternity, it seemed, as friends out of convenience. Little but our relatively similar personalities drew us too close to the other. Other friends were easier to connect with, to communicate with. We were never awkward, but we were never tied so close that we could see each other's flame. That little thing inside that made a person burn the way they should.

Until he started sharing his.

It was in little things, how he gave it to me. Piece by piece, each flame a gift for me to hold on to, for me to see the rest of his fire. He would offer silently to help me clean up after eating, working swiftly without a word. That was when I first received just a spark - the first spark I saw in his eyes. I held it in my heart, and always looked for his glowing eyes since.

Then, recognition. As I drowned in conversation - lost my foothold, lost my audience - he'd pull me back up to the surface. Another flame, just larger than the first spark appeared, and I began seeing it in his smile. I began seeing his fire grow. Flame after flame, small shards of his fire grew into my own personal flare as one I could hang on to every time we crossed paths. So that I could see that glow, that light, that shined within him every time we met.

I look at him again, his fire dancing in meticulous circles around his form. There's a calm in his fiery gaze, one that makes my heart crackle in my chest.

I never knew my own fire before - not until I met him.

As his eyes turn back to me, I feel it.

He starts a fire in my heart.

FEYTON OF THE AGES

The world was spinning.

Or no, was it my head? My eyes were shut tight, my head splitting with a dangerous headache. The world wasn't just spinning. Its details were groggy and useless to my scrambled brain. Even with my eyes closed as tight as humanly possible, everything moved and jumped and made me dizzy.

It was sickening.

I groaned and moved to press my hand to my forehead, but something held my hand in place. I tugged at whatever bound it, but it barely budged. I tried at my other hand and the same happened. I was trapped.

I opened my eyes slowly, doing my best to ignore the searing pain that split my head. What I saw was beyond disturbing. Or, maybe, hopefully, my scrambled brain just wasn't seeing things right.

Yes, that was it. That *had* to be it. If it wasn't, this was a living nightmare.

The first thing I noticed were the white walls, blinding if not for the very apparent splotches of blood in almost every nook and cranny near the floor, dried almost black. I found myself with my cheek pressed to the cold cement floor, both my hands tied in massive shackles that connected to the juncture between the back wall and floor. Straight across from me sat a single foldable chair, and behind it was a barely noticeable door with the tiniest reflective window.

Despite being shackled to the wall behind me, nothing else had been detained. My mouth was free of a gag, and if I tried, I could get to my feet without much struggle. No matter the freedom I was given, I was still tied to the ground by the shackles around my wrists.

What did I get myself into? I couldn't remember a single detail - not from the night before, not from the week before, not from seconds before I opened my eyes. The blinding white walls didn't help my head. Each glance sent tiny little pinpricks through my head every time I opened my eyes. My body was bruised and my clothing clung to my skin in a few places, like right below by diaphragm, as if soaked in my own blood. *I think I put up a fight then.* But I didn't feel pain.

Wait . . . why don't I feel pain?

"Because you're different, Feyton. The question is, do you know that and are hiding it from me or is it a mystery to you, too?"

That voice . . . I had heard it before. It floated up into my head, answering my own question yet leaving me with so many more. Where were my memories? Why couldn't I place a face to that voice? I had heard him before so clearly. The voice was unmistakable. It sparked a sense of nostalgia in me that only confused me more through my amnesia. Not a thing made sense the more I tried to find his face.

But those words moved in my head, and I did manage to place a time.

Last night.

I already had the suspicion that last night had been a complete mess by my, dare I say, bloody situation. But those words, the memory of that voice, still felt wrong in whatever the situation actually was.

I sat up slowly and pushed my back to the wall. I expected to wince as I moved, but yet again, no pain came. I opened my eyes and peered down at my stomach, not exactly surprised to find a huge, blood coated gash and a cut through my shirt soaked in red. It barely phased me, if I was honest. I knew it was there.

But why didn't I *feel* it?

"Because you're different, Feyton."

Shut up.

"They told me all about you. The worst part is, it makes sense. Everything you've done that was out of the ordinary, it makes sense with this. I can't believe I couldn't see it before now. You don't deserve what you've been given."

Please shut up.

"Save me," I had said. *"Please."*

"No."

The night came back to me in bunches of words, jumbled up conversations that sparked a sense of betrayal in me. A pain beyond anything I had felt before, a mental breaking. Not a physical pain. An emotional one, a strain on my trust. On my trust . . . in him.

Finally, *finally* his face gushed into my head. Not attractive but not ugly, not tall but not short, not small or large around the waist. He was average, with floppy brown hair and shining hazel eyes. He was lost as a memory of a kind person. An illusion. This face merged with the words looping around in my head, and I found myself surprised that tears were brought to my eyes.

I wanted him to save me.

I felt the ghost of hands around my waist and wrists, dragging me back, working to bruise my skin. Somehow, subconsciously, I knew no bruise would form no matter the pressure, but the feeling of the cold and clammy grip remained. I could do nothing. I had been immobilized, *drugged.* Even in this flashback the world was hazy, partially from my own tears and partially from my conscious slowly fading.

Maybe even partially from how broken I felt.

"No."

It was in low lighting - a soft red making the underside of his chin glow, the hazel of his eyes turn a hostile, searing blood red. A shining red. He pressed me to the floor as I strained to force myself up, saying "You're different, Feyton, you're different," and all I could do was cry. My trust shattered like glass. My heart did. Tears soaked the ground, running down my cheek as he kept my face flat against the ground, waiting for the drugs to act. I jolted up and ran into something sharp, gasping with a gurgle of blood as I hit a silver-sheened knife. I let out a broken sob, dropping to the ground again.

So that's where the blood came from.

I pulled myself up and wrapped my arms around my waist as far as the chains would let them. I rocked, realizing with another sting of shock that I was crying. Silently crying in memory of the past, squeezing my eyes shut and trying to make it stop.

"Because you're different, Feyton. The question is, do you know that and are hiding it from me or is it a mystery to you, too?"

I don't know. I really don't know.

Save me.

The drugs overtook me quickly.

And the memories of everything - of who I was, of who he was, of *why* - rushed back.

Feyton of the Ages, or rather, the Ageless Deity. She who feels no pain, who has no age, who only has memory of her reality when another finds it out first. She lived her life always young and free, and due to her nature, she never noticed as the world passed her by.

And he - her friend - West, he had discovered it. He had found the Ageless Deity, and he had not taken it well. Someone had known. Someone had told him of who I was, and the one person I could trust turned dark and lifeless in my eyes. We had been at a bar last night, and perhaps I was being naive when I noticed his pointed looks at the drinks and decided to ignore them, but the Ageless Deity had been felled that night by a dose of spiked alcohol. And into an alley he led us, away from the bar and into the shadows, to which I ignored again and wrote off, all until he pinned me to the ground and drew a knife.

"West!" I had screamed. Only a lost, human girl then, unaware of my title, I couldn't fathom why he'd do it. I thought he'd liked me. I thought we'd been friends. "What are you doing? W-why?"

Then the thing that had been circling and circling and circling.

"Because you're different, Feyton. The question is, do you know that and are hiding it from me or is it a mystery to you, too?"

It was a mystery to me, too, West. Why did you do it?

"They told me all about you. The worst part is, it makes sense. Everything you've done that was out of the ordinary, it makes sense with this. I can't believe I couldn't see it before now. You don't deserve what you've been given."

I don't know what I did to you.

"They promised a bounty for all you've done. You've apparently lived lives, Feyton, more than the world can supply. You've done things, things that are horrible. Horrible, horrible pasts. And you ask why?"

Of course I do. I can't remember any *of them.*

"Save me," I had pleaded. "Please."

I let out a broken sob once more. *"No."*

Everything faded to black all over again as the Ageless Deity submitted to blinding memories of the room.

And when she woke, Feyton the Ageless began a new life - a life of freedom, *worthy* of a bounty.

No one betrayed her trust again.

She made *sure* of that.

The Cycle of an Eternal

A Where the Worlds Meet Short

The days had begun to blur together.

Wake up, get ready, go to work, go home. The same cycle, spinning endlessly for weeks at a time. It was exhausting. There weren't any in-betweens. There weren't any changes. There wasn't a single thing new. It was all on repeat.

Over and over and over again.

Logan clutched his head as he hunched over his table, his tired eyes boring into the papers below him. A pen was tucked tight in one hand, his bent glasses snug in the other. Exhaustion pressed on his mind. He wanted to sleep. To forget. To ignore the world and take a few days to himself. But his cycle was still on repeat, and his days were ever-so-slowly changing into a single one. Upsetting the cycle wasn't worth his while.

He pulled his pen-hand down to the table as he focused squarely on his work. It was hard to see, but he couldn't tell if that was because of the pressure on his head or the dim yellow light to his left. He just could tell that he needed things done, things having to do with his low-paying office job, and he wasn't near motivated to do it. A surge of rage had him throwing the pen across the floor with an angered grunt.

Logan turned away as the pen flew airborne and pressed his forehead against his desk. He held himself there for a moment - a very long, very unproductive moment. As he pulled himself back up, though, he felt something.

A tremor.

An unnatural, vicious vibration rocked the ground, unlike anything he'd ever known.

Like it wasn't a pen that had just hit the ground.

Like something *else* had.

Dizziness crept up his neck. Placing a steadying hand on his desk, Logan swung his glasses back on his face and stood up to survey the room. That could *not* have been his pen. Whatever he felt, it shook with so much power that it had his mind vibrating along with it.

But nothing looked out of order when he glanced around. Nothing. His few pictures were still exactly where he left them, in their frames, on the walls. Everything on his desk was exactly as it was. Not a thing was out of place. Nothing was knocked over, collapsed on the floor, nor shattered or broken. And as he took in the rest of the room, it was the same as everything else.

Still stuck in the cycle. Unmoving.

He had to wonder if what he felt, only *he* felt.

Or if he had felt anything at all.

Logan balled his hands into fists. He wasn't thinking straight. Whatever that shaking that went through his mind was, it wasn't real. Not to the physical world, at least.

With a defeated sigh, he took his hallucination as a sign to turn in for the night.

As he began to clean up his messy desk, though, he paused. A change wafted in the air. He didn't know what, but he knew something was off. His lamp, still glowing its eerie yellow shine, flickered.

Once.

Twice.

Then off, dropping the house in an almost pure darkness. The only thing keeping it from the dark was a subtle blue glow from behind. Blinking slowly to adjust to the dimmer environment, he swung around to find it.

That was *not* there before.

He found it just under the sill of his window on the far wall of his house, nothing more than a condensed ball of light sitting on his carpet. That light - whatever it was - was far from natural. Far from normal.

But Logan could honestly care less.

If it could break the cycle, he'd take it.

When he did catch sight of the pale blue glow, it seemed to stare right back at him. Like it *wanted* him to know it was there. He couldn't describe it, couldn't place why he felt the way he did, but the light he found seemed like it was . . . alive. Pulsing and breathing and watching.

Or better yet, waiting.

And Logan was about to give it whatever it was waiting for.

In a single, unthinking stride, he reached out to the light -

And the cycle shattered.

Logan snapped his hand back as a cold wave flowed up through his arm from where he touched the light. It felt like freezing water ran up his veins, dunking his insides in an ice bath. His hand morphed, sucking in that cool blue glow, and soon his skin was gone - instead a hologram of light. The light engulfed him, and he was little more than a ghost. A thing of power, of freedom, of creation. His mind knew no limits, and his body no longer rooted him to the earth.

Flexing his muscleless form, he shot off the ground. He could feel no air as he pummeled through it, but he could feel that pulsing. Like a light within him, power of unbelievable measures beckoned to him. It collected between his fingers, through his arms, from his heart. It grew and grew, calling to his very being as he rocketed through time and space.

He could - and would - do anything.

Nothing was past his grasp.

Even that cycle, so obnoxiously stable, rocked off its tracks in his wake.

At a graze of that power, everything he hated and everything he loved turned unimportant. Greatness awaited him. Greatness and creation and destruction and rule. It all was before him, in that portal of time and space.

Feeling nothing and yet knowing everything, Logan let the unknown turn known in his new shapeless form. And years into his future, years and years and *years*, he still veered away from that cycle. Eternities passed him by. Worlds shaped by his own hand blossomed. That power pulsed like a star.

And yet, and yet, the cycle found him again.

It grabbed him by a tendril of his power, and once more, he felt that dose of cold. He drowned in the cycle, in the water of reality, and finally let himself sleep at the worry of facing that cycle again. He slept out of worry and mistrust and hopelessness. His mind fractured and torn, he stayed in that water and drowned as he slumbered.

He claimed a lake in one of his worlds and let it keep him still.

And when the time arose, he awoke.

Never again, not from that point forward, would he see that cycle. Would he live in it.

Not with his world fighting to end it too.

Not with the powers of Aurielle on his side.

—The Forebody

The Fault in a Feeling

Potential Teaser

Reading was a nifty tool. Being literate? Sure, if you really wanted to pursue that kind of thing. But reading people was something that had more pros than cons in the end. Treating yourself, your emotions, your *life* as a moldable slate was even more so, if you could read right. I understood that. Control was one of the belittled elements of a conversation. Emotion was important to maintain a good discussion. But if that control was utilized so that emotion seemed to be there when it really wasn't, who would notice the difference?

No one. Not even yourself.

From a young age, I'd used being essentially emotionless to oppress the feelings I no longer wanted to experience - or rather, all of them. It had become my second nature. There - a twitch in her brow. She was hiding something, covering up how she truly felt about the topic. Or oh, the slightest slouch, he's no longer interested. Even the quiver of their lip, the slightest skip in their step, menial things that no other person wanted to look for - I saw it all.

I used it all.

Then, finally, when it came to it, I would turn it back on them.

Mirroring emotions turned out to be just as easy as reading them. Of course, after ignoring myself for so long, I kind of . . . lost it. With nothing left but the copied emotions of others, I had no personality. No life separate from others. No cares save for perfection. I pushed down my emotions, so I pushed myself down.

I hadn't known who I truly was in a long, long time.

And I fully intended to stay that way.

The cool of November seemed to seep into my bones. A chilly breeze licked my cheek, a remnant of the latest snow. I sat bundled in a thin winter jacket on a bench just outside of my school, tired but careful to not show it. My posture was practiced. I gave myself enough slouch to pass as unnoticeable and kept to a blank stare, just enough to watch and track the world without drawing attention. I had to keep my eyes and mind open at all times. Should anything pass me, I could break.

And I *never* broke.

I squeezed my hand when I just missed the movement behind me, the voice that rolled thick like honey. "Brianne."

My eyes snapped back. I found myself staring up at exactly who I'd expected - December, the raven haired petite heartthrob for the junior class. Not quite an ignorant one either, even though she tried to play it off that way. December knew how her looks sent boys swooning, and while she did her best to follow in my footsteps and ignore the reality, she absentmindedly used their fascination to her advantage. Blamed it on her "irresistible attitude."

Irresistible indeed.

"Hello, December," I droned, tearing my eyes away from her.

"Quit it, you insufferable rock. Look at me," she said. She had a kind of fire in her eyes.

Insufferable rock. December's nickname for me. It was quite fitting, actually. December was a train wreck of emotions, and hanging out with me even the tiniest bit - essentially a shell to other people - drove her mad. I learned to quit showing emotions years ago, even to my own family.

I wasn't about to make exceptions for a dramatic social butterfly.

I crossed my legs and tipped my head up to the dark haired brunette. Her eyes blazed.

"*Thank you*," December mumbled through gritted teeth. She flicked a strand of hair behind her shoulder and held my gaze. December then set one gloved hand on my shoulder and let out a strained sigh. "Sooooo, Bri, Griffin's family has a big bonfire going on at the lake tonight, and he asked me to go, buuuuuut . . ." December trailed off, ever so slightly smirking. Her eyebrows waggled.

I changed my expression just enough so it seemed like my interest was piqued. A quirked brow, wider eyes. Then, in a higher pitched voice for December's amusement, I asked, "But?"

December smiled wider. "But I don't wanna go alone."

"You won't be. Griffin will be there," I said.

"Bri, I want you to come with," December grumbled. "C'mon, it won't kill you! Please? For me?"

I don't know what it was that possessed me to agree, but I did. December would always ask me to come with her to these things - these chaotic social events. My continual answer was no. When I was around large groups of people, controlling my responses got more difficult. I couldn't please everyone, nor could I read everyone. Social events were never worth my while for that reason.

But whatever it was that possessed me to go, I chose not to dwell on it.

The air that night was freezing. It didn't have that familiar chill from snow - it had that evil, sharp bite of Jack Frost when you wake up in the mornings and realize everything needs defrosting. It was what brought me closer to the big bonfire in the middle of the crowd and closer to the loud racket of barbecuing. I acted like December's tail, not missing a step following behind the pretty brunette as she chatted up the whole party.

I was only a shadow. I preferred it that way.

December flitted from person to person before she finally settled next to her long-term boyfriend, Griffin. They were a cute couple, like two halves of the same whole. What one fell short in, the other made up for. They were an interesting pair to watch, too. Their body language immediately fell in sync whenever they got close to one other, and as time went on, their moods started doing the same.

Griffin rested on an old, messy hay bale near the bonfire on the opposite side of the commotion with his back pressed up against a fragile tree. His blonde hair flayed out in a chaotic spiral around his head. He wore a tight navy sweatshirt to ward off the cold, too big around his wrists. Next to him on another hay bale was a slightly taller, thicker built guy with a mop of feathered brown hair on his head, dipping just over his eyebrows. He leaned over his knees with his elbows pressed against his thighs, a glorious grin shining as he chatted with Griffin.

When my eyes first stopped on him, something felt wrong. I mentally shook it off, trying to ignore the twinge in my chest.

"Griffiiiiiiin!" December called as she skipped over to her boyfriend's hay bale and scooted in beside him. I strolled up behind her and paused before the bales, taking in how Griffin's face brightened at the sight of his girl.

"Hey, Deci," Griffin said. He wrapped one arm around December and pulled her into the curve of his side until she looked snug against him. "I haven't seen you all night! Bri, you can sit next to Reece if you want."

The fluffy haired boy looked up to me at the mention of his name with a twinkle in his coffee-brown eyes.

That moment - that menial, typically unimportant moment - was when I truly felt it.

Yes, *felt* it.

He gave me a brilliant smile and formally introduced himself, but

I didn't hear it. My ears felt clogged. I tried to read him instead, to judge who he was and what gutted me as I looked at him. I tried so very hard, but no matter what I did, he seemed impossible. I knew he wasn't like me, emotionless and conditioned to be so, because I could see the happiness on his face. All the same, I couldn't see past his face-value. I couldn't see past the white-toothed smile, or the glow in his eyes, or the crinkle in his brow.

Stars glittered in my vision.

I swallowed down the uneasiness in my stomach. I tried to give him a curt nod and a small smile for greeting, a typical neutral hello, but my body decided against listening. Instead heat flooded to my cheeks in a violent wave. I turned away from him, suddenly relieved that the nail-biting cold gave me an out.

What in the world is happening to me?

I tried to play it off, running one hand through my coarse bob of ash brown hair as I sat as far as possible from Reece on the bale. Night settled over us like a heavy cloud. It gave the fire a cozy, ominous glow. The heat in my cheeks wouldn't subside as the bonfire went on, and it only got worse every time I felt Reece's gaze fall on me. My heart felt caged in my chest, beating against self-inflicted bars. I decided, in my best interest, to keep my mouth shut should any more unexpected emotions slip.

Just ignore it, I told myself. *Just ignore it.*

The feeling tripled when December started talking to Reece. I had been struggling ever since we sat down to keep whatever it was that was bothering me in check, but seeing December - a flawless, beautiful girl in sharp contrast to my mangled, careless physique - simply talk to Reece brought on another emotion.

Jealousy.

I was *jealous.*

I bit down on my teeth. My eyes squeezed shut. My head felt like it was splitting with the tidal wave of feelings. I couldn't handle it. I couldn't handle another second. Everything that was once in my grasp this morning had slipped completely, and somehow, it was all because of this grinning boy beside me.

His watch found me, and I couldn't hold on.

I didn't even give myself time to think as I shot up from the bale and backed away from the group. Their conversation had been a jumble of useless words to me anyway. I couldn't even read December or Griffin anymore, arguably the easiest people to read, especially when together.

December looked startled. I didn't know if she was. I couldn't tell. She just looked it. " . . . Bri?"

"December, I- I need to go." I tripped over my words. I *never* tripped over my words.

December's eyes widened, and Griffin's stare narrowed. Reece only watched. He didn't know who I was. He'd never notice what just happened.

He'd never know that I just broke.

"Bri?" December asked again. Her eyes trailed over to Griffin's, and she said something with her look that he seemed to understand. I didn't know what. Maybe I could've, if I weren't broken. *Oh no, why isn't anything making sense?* December got up and gave Griffin a light peck on the cheek, then slipped next to me and looped her arm around mine. "I'm your ride, Bri. You can't go without me. I'll see you tomorrow, Griff. You too, Reece." I swallowed down a growing feeling of emptiness.

I've always known I was empty, but I've never *felt* it before. Especially not in front of others - never in front of others. I've never felt a fear of letting myself go before either. I was incapable of feeling those fears. I made myself that way.

He undid every lock I put in place.

"Drive safe," was all Griffin said. Reece's watchful eyes hovered over me, a barely audible "bye" as his farewell. Finally, finally, I turned away from him.

I sucked in a breath of that icy air again and let December guide me to her car. I didn't look at her or her obvious confusion. I didn't need to to know it was there.

I had just broken. I had broken, shattered and snapped, and from the look of the near future . . . I closed my eyes.

From the look of the near future, there didn't seem to be any fixing in sight.

Morphers Short Stories

Potential Teasers

The next stories are all based in the same world, a fantasy concept known as the Morphers. In this world, creatures are able to switch between two forms, a feral and a humanoid. Creatures known as Castervillains, or Defect Morphers, switch between two feral. Allforms are as they suggest, those who can harbor any form they want so long as they know it exists - though these Morphers are reportedly rare.

Each story follows a point in a determined storyline.

Tyto Alba and Kelpie

It was her first Gathering.

Granted, it wasn't her first Gathering where she had to *do* something, but it was still awkward. Only leaders were allowed at Gatherings. And one time, and one time only, their apprentice was allowed to come and survey.

And tonight was Tyto Alba's night. Her introduction to true leadership.

It was scary.

It was new.

It was eye-opening.

Tyto Alba wrung her hands as she stood next to Blanc, an addax Morpher, or rather, her mentor. Blanc was more commonly known as Dunesear's leader - powerful and wise, but bright and colorful. The perfect mentor for Tyto Alba.

Among the Dunesear residents were Forestlie's leader, Lacertilia, and the leader of Chillmount, Eisbar. Tyto Alba snuck glances at them every so often, but she was scared they'd catch her gaze, which frightened her more than she wanted to admit. They stood with a powerful and demanding aura, both of them, and they freaked Tyto Alba out. But she may just have to get used to it if Blanc . . . left before either of them did.

There was also the leader of Skywake, Ursus, lingering to the side, but he made no effort to talk to Blanc, Tyto Alba, or the other leaders. Tyto Alba didn't mind, really - she wasn't the social type, but the way he loomed in the shadows felt a little off-putting considering the Gatherings were designed to maintain peace.

And he did not look particularly peaceful.

"Why are you so tense, Alba?" It took Tyto Alba a moment to realize Blanc had spoken to her. Her mind was a little preoccupied.

"Sorry," Tyto Alba said, reaching back to muffle the feathers on the crown of her head. She still held some feathers from her owl form in her human one, and she treated them like hair. Capable of being styled, of being redesigned every day, for every outfit. A fashion sense, in her mind. "It's a little nerve wracking here, if I'm honest. To be alone with the leaders . . ."

Blanc let out a small, lighthearted chuckle. "You spend time with me every day," he pointed out.

"Well, yes," Tyto Alba murmured. "But I'm used to you. They're all so scary." She gestured primarily to Eisbar and Lacertilia. They paid no attention to her, luckily.

"Ah," Blanc mused, catching her drift. "Pay no mind to them, then. We're all equals here, remember? Leader or not, this is a place of peace. Not . . . *awkwardness.*" Blanc grumbled a laugh again, and Tyto Alba had to join him. *This* was why Tyto Alba was proud to have Blanc as her leader and mentor. He wasn't afraid to laugh.

"What is so amusing, you two?" Eisbar asked as his cold blue-green eyes thinned on the Dunesear Morphers. Despite Blanc's reassurance, Tyto Alba still tensed once more. It thickened when Lacertilia's eyes flicked over to them, too.

Blanc saved her from having to answer. "Nothing much really. Just some lighthearted conversation." Blanc flashed a grin.

Lacertilia smiled back, but it almost looked evil. Tyto Alba returned the smile rather weakly. The Forestlie leader was just being courteous, but she still scared the ever-loving daylights out of Tyto Alba.

The conversation slowly grew brighter, but Tyto Alba still refused to participate. She was here to watch and observe. She didn't have to speak with the Morphers who made her whole body shiver in fear. It would've been nice, yes, for her to overcome this irrational fear. But she'd act on it another time, another time when she *needed* to.

So she just sat and watched.

That was, until a certain Morpher walked into the Gatherplace.

Some time had passed, enough to warrant the yawn Tyto Alba fought growing in her throat, when the final two Morphers walked side by side into the clearing. One of them, she noted, looked like he had just gotten a bucket of water thrown at him. The dripping composure made sense, though, as Tyto Alba realized the creature who walked in was a shimmering black kelpie.

Tyto Alba barely noticed the small fox that slinked in next to him. She only caught sight of the kelpie, step after step oozing with a confidence she could only wish to have. And a feeling, an odd and uncontrollable feeling, crept right into Tyto Alba's heart. A flutter. A small, meaningless-at-the-time flutter, but it was there. It was making up her mind. Forming a relationship, an attachment to this creature. And when he transformed into a pale-skinned man with dark wavy locks that brushed his collarbone, the fluttering got louder. Brighter. Faster.

Scarier.

That time, Tyto Alba felt it.

She clutched her heart, hoping it would go away. It didn't. It stayed. And the kelpie Morpher noticed. All he did was smile at her, though - a beautiful, radiant smile, almost like he had found a connection with Tyto Alba too. She foolishly hoped so. But then and again, she didn't.

Morphers weren't *allowed* to date in between kingdoms. It was forbidden, especially for leaders. If a leader's focus was divided and they cared too heavily for another, their own kingdom could suffer.

But the beating in Tyto Alba's heart was overpowering, and before she knew it, the man had appeared right in front of her.

"Hello," he greeted her in a sharp but gurgly kind of accent. She liked it. "I'm Kelpie."

Tyto Alba hated the way she swooned when he said it. She cleared her throat nervously. "Tyto Alba, wonderful to meet you." Her hand shook as she offered it to him. Viciously.

He took it and gave it a good shake. "Same to you. To whom do you accompany?"

Tyto Alba straightened her back, trying her best to *not* do something irrevocably stupid. "Leader of Dunesear, Blanc."

Kelpie grunted in reply, but a smile snaked across his lips. Tyto Alba smiled bashfully.

"What a surprise," he murmured, his white eyes scanning her up and down. Tyto Alba ignored the way her body reacted. Her mind was not as disciplined. "We weren't expecting to see you for another moon."

"Oh?" Tyto Alba's voice vibrated, but she did her best to hold firm.

"Just something Blanc . . . seemed to hint at, at the last Gathering. Nothing special. You just missed Eisbar's successor, though, I'm afraid." Kelpie informed her, suddenly examining his nails all too closely. "She came last moon."

Tyto Alba's heart sank as he said it. *She.* Was there another? But when his eyes flicked up and met hers again, Tyto Alba knew there wasn't. There was some sort of understanding that dawned in his eyes, no matter their lifeless nature. But his eyes weren't lifeless to Tyto Alba - they were wildly full of emotion and wonder, and she couldn't help wanting to hold his stare until the sun came up.

But that would've been awkward. And they'd just met.

She broke eye contact.

"The more, the worse, for me," Tyto Alba admitted. "The smallest group is the best group in my opinion."

"I suppose that does make sense," Kelpie purred. He ever so slightly blew his hair out of his right eye, but it flopped back into place. He didn't seem to care.

Tyto Alba squirmed a bit before she said, "No big groups for you either?"

"Ah, not exactly great at connecting with others, more like it," he responded. "The less there are, the less unnecessary formalities, I suppose. Why do you ask?"

"I feel like you're fine at connecting."

Kelpie laughed. "I don't think it's me that's fine at connecting. You made it a little easier. If that makes sense." He pivoted slightly to the side. "I meet everyone else so formally. You, well, you are different."

"I-I didn't mean to be informal," Tyto Alba stuttered, wanting to smack herself on the head for forgetting her formality lessons with Blanc. Kelpie looked like he wanted to answer, maybe playfully, but-

"Kelpie," Eisbar's gravelly voice hissed. "The Gathering is starting."

Kelpie blinked slowly and turned to Eisbar with a slight nod. Then, he turned back to Tyto Alba and smiled. A small smirk or a big grin, either or. She couldn't tell if her vision was warping, or if he just could pull that off. "I enjoy you, Tyto Alba." He leaned in, and Tyto Alba's cheeks flamed. She could feel his breath near her cheek when he whispered, "I know this is outside of kingdom regulations, but I really do like you. I'd like to meet you again." Then he pulled away and strolled up to Eisbar, winking at Tyto Alba.

And Tyto Alba stood there, lost in thought, and probably red from head to toe.

She didn't hear a word or see a thing that happened at the Gathering. Her mind was on Kelpie.

And what he said.

"I'd like to meet you again." That's what he said. And he did.

They met every night after, at the Narroway stream. They grew closer at each hidden meeting, on each illegal date. They even ended up calling it official. Dating. Together.

Who knew it could go just as horribly wrong as all kingdom regulations suggested?

Astraeus and Lacertilia

The hair on Lacertilia's arms had stood on end all day. Something was off, or at least, bound to be eventually. The Naming had been last night, and it was always a sense of joy to her and her people whenever Forestlie was gifted a new creature. Nothing *should* feel off about the day after a Naming.

But it did.

Lacertilia knew better than to ignore senses like these, too. A power that came within a basilisk's territory was a kind of sense that radiated from her head like a mental power, something that protected her from creatures who had the ability to toggle with her mind. Better yet, this sense warned her of incidents before they happened. It wasn't special and it was often just a feeling with no context, but she never, *never* ignored it. She couldn't afford to.

Lacertilia sat in her Dwellinghouse with blank eyes, too rattled by this feeling to work. It was more aggressive than the other times she'd felt it - a violent feeling that rattled in her chest. It was sickening.

What was even more sickening was knowing that whatever caused this was near.

Lacertilia rubbed her temples. Her head was throbbing. She nearly jumped out of her skin when she heard footsteps, quickly followed by a dark sneer, and the subtle, quiet sound of breathing.

The breathing was off. Lacertilia focused on it, taking what she could from it. She wouldn't move from her spot or infuriate this threat. She would be casual. She would allow whoever it was to believe she was unaware of their presence. But the breathing she was hearing, it was neither labored nor normally inconsistent - it was slow and mindless. There were multiple creatures, and at least one of them was not awake.

Mentally awake, that is. At least one of the creatures outside her Dwellinghouse was being controlled.

"Motherstar and beyond," Lacertilia swore.

She couldn't even fathom what a Morpher of that power would be doing outside her Dwellinghouse. She wasn't the eldest, so she had no control or power over the other leaders. Nothing out of the ordinary had happened in Forestlie in a good, long while. So why would a mind-manipulator be outside her Dwellinghouse?

Lacertilia's eyes flashed red. Her mind calmed down immediately.

A creak sounded over her shoulder, and, acting oblivious, Lacertilia let herself glance back. The door was open just a smidgen. A face poked his way through the crack in the doorway, long white hair framing his youthful face. He was charming, in a sense, with a chiseled jawline and strong, piercing gray eyes, but his presence in itself was overwhelming.

This creature - this Morpher - he is the threat.

The man's eyes skipped to Lacertilia, and doing her best not to miss it, Lacertilia caught the subtle flicker in his expression. The moment he aimed to claim Lacertilia's mind. A firewall, of sorts, slammed into place in Lacertilia's mind, blocking out his commands. She turned her head away from him, though, in the effort to give him the illusion that she was as mindless as whomever he brought with him. A trick of Lacertilia's own doing, in a sense.

As soon as Lacertilia's gaze latched onto the opposite wall of the mind-manipulator, she heard the shuffle of creatures entering her home. It was quiet, but Lacertilia could pick up three sets of feet, two quadrupeds and one biped - the white-haired man.

A sigh sounded, ricocheting off the walls of her Dwellinghouse, and Lacertilia didn't even flinch when the white-haired man's voice sliced through the air.

"Shh, Cervy," he snapped. The movement stopped. "Let's get this over with. Turn."

Lacertilia's eyes flickered red. Another intrusion, another blocking. He told her to turn, so she did, breathing as little life into her expression as possible.

It was then that she saw the other creatures. Without moving her eyes, she took in the helpless creatures under the man's control. One was a pure deer, with delicate limbs and a knife-sharp face etched with a permanently worried expression. The second was also a deer, a tiny bit smaller than the first, but unlike the normal forest creature, this one had wings. They were huge, white wings that offset his appearance, way too bright and bold for his tan-speckled coat. His features were scarily similar to the first deer. They were likely related.

What an odd turn of events.

Under the impression that no one was in the right mind to understand him, the man began speaking. "You've caused me too much trouble, Cervy. It wasn't supposed to happen like this. Not even with this little nuisance." Lacertilia stayed still as a rock as the man gestured towards the younger winged deer with an aggravated snarl. "Let's just hope you don't screw up any lives inside the walls of society."

"Astraeus?" Her voice was weak, but Lacertilia could tell it was truly hers. She had woken. The older deer craned her head to either side with wide, sad eyes. "Where are we? Veado, is that you?" The young deer didn't move, didn't blink, didn't respond. "Astraeus?"

The white-haired man, Astraeus, turned to her slowly. "Cervy," he said leisurely. Cervy flinched back.

The deer reached one hoof forward towards Astraeus, but made no move further. Astraeus's expression stayed neutral, even bordering on annoyed.

"What's going on, Ast?" Her voice shook.

"I'm saying goodbye." Cervy's gaze turned to a lifeless-looking Lacertilia and her brow furrowed into a frown, taking in the man's words.

"Goodbye? What is this? That's- that's the Forestlie leader . . . why are we here, Astraeus?"

Cervy retreated from the white-haired man and morphed as she made her way over to the winged deer, Veado. She was a light-haired brunette with a slim figure and the ghost of bones under her wrists, thin as paper. Her hair was pulled up into a messy bun, drooping to the left, and her eyes were just as tired and worried as before. She cupped the young deer's face in her palms and scanned his lifeless form, tracing one thumb down his cheek.

Astraeus sighed and leaned forward, towards Cervy, as the hint of regret flashed over his face. "My blossom, I'm sorry. I can't go on like this anymore. These last fifteen years . . . they've been subpar, to say the very least. I know that I have more in store for myself, and I need to return to where I've come from if I'm to maintain it. I can't have any distractions anymore, though. I must leave you."

"And this is how you decided to leave? You promised you wouldn't do this to us, Ast."

He turned away. "If this goes correctly, that won't matter, blossom. You won't remember."

One hand still on Veado's face, Cervy turned around to face Astraeus with another frown. "What's that supposed to mean, Astraeus?"

"I think you know," he droned. "I just have to finish with the Forestlie leader and you'll be all set."

"*Astraeus!*" Cervy screeched, eyes wild. A single tear slipped out as her rigid posture returned. She was gone again.

Astraeus sighed and swiveled away from Lacertilia to face the young deer that Cervy held so close. As he let out a breath, Veado's eyes grew lively and he turned to find Astraeus, confused.

"Dad?" He asked.

"Veado, no. Astraeus, kid," he replied as he pinched his brow.

"What's happening?" He asked, stepping one hoof towards Cervy and stifling an all-too-frequent frown.

Astraeus closed his eyes. "Nothing. My son, I just need you to remember. I'll be away from you and your mother, and when you're of age or when you've done something to prove yourself, come find me. You'll do things no one else can fathom when the time comes." Then Veado snapped back to a lost soul. "It's too bad I have to leave you two behind." Astraeus pressed his fingers onto his son's temples.

The light in Veado's eyes diminished. He then turned to Cervy and repeated the process, her eyes turning dull and lost as well. Astraeus finally turned to Lacertilia.

His fingers were cold as he pressed them to Lacertilia's own temples. His gray eyes flashed blue, and the change in his expression hinted at yet another intrusion. Lacertilia willed her eyes to stay normal even if it made the process of keeping him out more difficult. The firewall, despite being weaker, slid right back into place. Lacertilia intentionally left a hole in it, though, just enough to understand what he was trying to enforce on her mind.

Lacertilia choked on a stalled gasp. Images more powerful than she'd ever felt before slipped through the hole, first of the past, and then covering those images with a fake reality.

Astraeus was a *god*. An Allform with an immortal life. By chance, he found Cervy, and together they had the boy kid Veado. A merge of Morpher and Allform. A freak of nature that not even an immortal Allform could predict. The white haired man was scared of his offspring. He was scared for his life.

New images fuzzed into place over the top of the ones given.

Cervy was a Naming born creature, many moons old, and had an old lover who died unexpectedly. *Not true*, Lacertilia's mind whispered over the images. The lover was a pegasus Morpher from Skywake. The two never had the opportunity to have a child, so Veado, also a Naming born, was made an exception and given to Cervy as a son. They have no relation. They have no relation. *Not true.*

Astraeus let go of Lacertilia's head. The intrusion was over.

Then the Allform snapped, and Lacertilia heard a single command. *Sleep.* Veado and Cervy, blank-eyed and loose-limbed, collapsed to the floor at the snap. Lacertilia mirrored them, allowing herself to limply fall out of her chair. With a satisfied grunt, Astraeus left Lacertilia's home with his disowned family still crumpled on the ground.

When the feeling of danger died down and Lacertilia's mind let go of the firewall, she pushed herself off the ground and shuffled over to the two deer Morphers. She let out a sigh of relief when both of them had steady and healthy heartbeats. The two of them were out cold, but no damage had been done to them in the memory wipe.

It took some work, but Lacertilia got Cervy, still in her human form, onto Lacertilia's bed and moved Veado onto a cushioned mat nearby. She'd make the arrangements. She'd tell them what the Allform wanted them to know, at least until they were ready. She would treat the abandoned family as Morphers of Forestlie, but she would always watch for their threat.

This time it wasn't simply a feeling.

The immortal Allform had some purpose, some goal, and it involved the winged deer currently asleep in her room.

He was going to come back.

Young Veado and Kirin

She wasn't certain she'd find him here, but she had a good hunch.

She moved slowly towards a large tree with a wide trunk and long, sturdy limbs that seemed to reach down to the ground as if it were offering someone a ride. To the naked eye, it *was* sturdy. It was thick and strong and huge. But few actually knew that this tree was only strong on the outside, for on the inside it was hollow, and Kirin's favorite playplace.

Well, Kirin and Veado's.

It only had been a couple weeks since they met, but they already knew each other like the back of their hands. Maybe even better. And Kirin couldn't be more proud. Her days with her Sharehouse partners had begun to turn dull and boring, all up until a few weeks back when a lean deer with some of the sharpest features Kirin had ever seen walked into their Dwellinghouse - with him.

He was an average sized boy with skinny arms and features similarly sharp as his caretaker. His fluffy hair poofed around his ears like a wild storm and deer antlers jutted out of his head. He looked all too much like his Sharehouse partner to the point where Kirin began to believe she was his mother, but he had assured her she wasn't. Kirin wasn't so sure she believed that.

He did have wings though, odd large feathered wings. But Kirin didn't mind. Something new, something . . . *exciting* had just walked into her life, and she wasn't about to let it go.

Besides, he was kinda cute.

And so they became friends. Best friends, actually. Kirin couldn't deny the pounding in her chest whenever she saw him either. Something else, some different feeling was stirring. For fear of it not being returned, though, she pushed it down until she couldn't find it. But it always came back up and messed with her head. She just had to ignore it.

Kirin knocked on the wood as quietly as she could to avoid any unwanted attention. She had chosen to ignore the frantic screaming coming from Veado's Dwellinghouse, where the tree was closest to. His Sharehouse partner had been outside looking for him for what seemed like a while, but just like Kirin, all he wanted to do was get away. So Kirin tried once more, and finally a shaky breath came from the tree.

"Kirin?"

"I thought you'd never answer, geez," Kirin muttered. When no response came, she continued, "Get out, c'mon. Let's go to the pond."

"Cervy may see me," Veado answered from within the tree.

Kirin clicked her tongue, knowing he was talking about his Sharehouse partner. "She won't."

An almost silent rustling occurred, and finally a little poofy haired boy popped his head out from the trunk just above a thick branch. Kirin looked up to find him smiling, eyes trailing about her golden hair. He almost looked like he was gawking. At *her*, even. But they were friends, and nothing more. So he couldn't have been.

"She's not there?" He asked, dipping his head.

"No, Veado," Kirin mumbled. "I . . . figured something out today. You'll like it. It'll keep her distracted, okay?"

Veado nodded and climbed his way down the tree. When he met Kirin at the bottom, he smiled. "You figured something out? What?"

"Hor- unicorn stuff. Magic." Kirin fidgeted with her hair, hating the swelling feeling rising in her chest. She nudged the pendant around her neck and watched it emit a brilliant pink light, turning her from human to unicorn. "Morph! C'mon! If we ever wanna get there, we're gonna have to use four legs instead of two."

Veado paused and looked at his wings. "Cervy's gonna be sending the whole of Forestlie after me. If I go deer, she'll find me too easily with these stupid things." At that, he fluttered the hunks of feathers. Kirin had to admit he had a point.

"W-would it be too awkward if I let you ride on my back?" Kirin asked as her shimmering white body twitched. There's the feeling again.

"Of course not!" And Veado did his best to climb on her back, very, very, *very* slowly. And if anyone asked Kirin, very awkwardly too.

Kirin practically rushed to the small shimmering pond that they frequented. It was basically the in-between point of their Dwelling-houses, a place where they could easily meet up without venturing too far. She was jittery with the cute boy clinging to her mane. She needed to get him off as soon as possible. When they hit the pond, she could tell Veado felt similar, because he immediately slid off her back before she even stopped walking.

"So, what was it that you actually learned?" Veado asked as Kirin returned to her human form.

"Illusions," she answered. Veado plopped down at the edge of the lake, and Kirin followed. "If I try hard enough, I can make an object look a lot like something else. But it takes a lot." Kirin's hand moved to her horn, and she made it flicker with a white glow to demonstrate. "Magic is hard."

"And your mentor, has he been helping?" Veado asked, dipping his head to her.

Kirin thought back to her magic mentor, a chimera Morpher. She'd told Veado about him every so often, but it was a touchy subject for her. She didn't get to spend nearly as much time with her Sharehouse partners because of the magic she bore. And she wasn't much of a fan of Trix.

"Trying," was all Kirin answered with. She cocked her head to look at her friend, and her eyes drifted to his wings. "What about you? Any luck with those wings?"

Veado fidgeted and flicked the tips of his feathers. "No. No winged quadrupeds around so . . . no luck."

Kirin heaved a sigh. "If only Trix had wings, then we could suffer through his lessons together."

He laughed. "I don't think I'd *want* to be a part of Trix's lessons."

"No," Kirin agreed, "you definitely don't."

The unicorn Morpher paused before glancing over at her friend again, then back to the glittering pond.

"Y'know, Forestlie is a little annoying in that sense, I guess. We've got a lot of animals that are grounded. I wonder - do you think maybe, if you asked Lacertilia about it, that she may try and set up a tutor to help you from Skywake?" Kirin asked him.

Veado sounded like he nearly choked. "Skywake?"

"Yeah," Kirin said. "Pegasi."

That was all she said, but that was also all she needed to say. She knew Veado. She knew he'd understand. Skywake had the leading population of pegasus Morphers. They, in Kirin's opinion, were the closest option Veado had to learning how to fly with feathered wings. Kirin still knew, though, that no matter how much she pushed him to learn, he still didn't trust himself to believe he could do it.

"I don't think Lacertilia would have a problem with an arrangement like that, would you?" Kirin pressed.

Veado shook his head, but wouldn't meet Kirin's eyes. Instead, he took off his shoes and dipped his feet in the pond. "Of course she wouldn't. I just . . . don't know if I'm ready."

Kirin scoffed. "If I'm ready to train with *Trix* of all Morphers, you'd be beyond ready to train with a foreigner."

"But I've never met someone from Skywake! I wouldn't know how to act around them!" Veado shot back.

"They're normal Morphers, just like you and me." Kirin growled.

"*I don't want to learn to fly yet, Kirin,*" Veado snapped, tearing his hand through his hair and stepping away from her. Kirin reached out to grab him, to *stop* him, but paused before she touched him. He sulked over to a tree and pressed his hand against it, hanging his head.

"I know you're trying to help," he whispered. "But I don't think I *want* to fly, not just yet. I told you, I'm not ready."

"No," Kirin mused, leaning back on her hands and tearing her gaze away from Veado. She couldn't bear to look at him, not when he was so defeated. "I know you. I know that you *are* ready. And I don't mean that to be pushy-" Kirin quickly corrected when she saw Veado wheel around to deliver a rebuttal. "*But*, you're scared. And I would be too. To get what you need, you'd really have to jump some serious hurdles. But you can do it. I know you can. I won't say you have to do it now, no matter how good it would be for you if you did, I'm just saying you've been ready for this way longer than you think."

Veado stood there, jaw tight as he worked through his response. "Thanks."

It was nervous, and bashful, and to Kirin so cute Motherstar would've fallen over blushing, but he said it. And it made Kirin's heart flutter and beat so loudly she had to pull her gaze away from his again. Take a deep breath. Remind herself of their actual relationship, and the problem at hand. Not *crushes*.

"Anytime, really." Kirin smiled, knowing her answer was definite.

Veado knew it too.

Neither of them knew just how far those small words would truly end up going.

MANTICON'S ESCAPE

He was running.

Manticon ran so hard that the wind stole his breath and his lungs strained against his chest. Did he want to run? No. Any creature that had wings would love to choose flight over feet. But Manticon would risk everything and then some if he tried to use his wings, so feet were the only option. They hid him, they carried him - the only thing they didn't do was make him feel comfortable.

But comfort was a long shot when running from his kingdom, so he'd just have to get over it.

Monty listened to the thrum of his heart and the beat of his steps, powering forward as fast as he could. He could hear them, smell them, even see them at some points. The Defects chasing him.

To think of his own kind as Defects sickened Monty to the point where he felt he may need to stop and just hurl. But those following *weren't* his kind. They followed the Castervillain king, the corrupt king. So referring to those creatures behind him as anything other than Defect would be wrong. They'd defected themselves. They were Defects regardless.

Manticon heard wingbeats just above him, and he halted as quickly as he could. Giving himself away would be just as stupid as turning around and saying "I'm sorry I betrayed you, oh corrupt king. Please don't hurt me." Manticon knew better. He ducked his head and slowly merged into the leaves behind him, trying his best to hide himself. But Manticon wasn't small - in fact, he was actually quite large being a manticore - so he could only hope that the Defects were blind.

The wingbeats remained, and he hoped that the creature above him was anything but a roc. If it were a roc, a bird of prey larger than life, he'd come himself. The corrupt king. At that point, Manticon was doomed.

"Manticon of Castervile, come out!" The winged creature demanded. "I can smell you!"

Two more sets of wingbeats came into hearing range. Two more creatures. Monty dropped lower.

Lucky for him, the voice wasn't the king's. It was deeper and raspier, and sounded like the kind of voice that even the strongest and mightiest cowered to. Monty's ears twitched towards the voice. It was too risky now to run. He'd finally get to use his wings.

As quietly as possible, Manticon crept forward, tucked his wings close, and dared himself to look up at the winged followers. None of them looked like a roc, so that made Monty feel over the moon about this escape. There was a smallish dragon with three curly, jagged horns and an oversized griffin who looked like she'd lived at least 100 years. He knew griffin Morphers could, so it didn't surprise him. The fact that the griffin was a Defect surprised him more.

The last one, the raspy voice that demanded he reveal himself, was a massive manticore like Manticon. That scared him. This manticore had to have lived longer than the griffin, probably near 200 to 250 years old. His size suggested it. He had a jagged scar over his right eye and long, serrated claws. His wings had gigantic tears that flapped and shuttered with each wingbeat, but he gave no mind to it. All he watched was the ground.

And to Monty's disdain, the runaway Castervillain.

"There you are." He smirked as Manticon flew from his hiding spot and shot forward.

He pushed himself harder with each beat and finally took to the sky. The Defects followed him relentlessly.

All I have to do is get to the Allform kingdom, Manticon thought hopefully. He'd never believe that all of the Allform royalty was completely killed off. He couldn't. He'd *warned* the princess about the plan to overthrow the Allforms. He'd told her everything, and he had to trust that she did what she could to escape. But the king came back triumphant that night and told the entirety of Castervile that he'd succeeded. That Allform royalty was dead.

But Monty still wouldn't believe it.

Manticon pushed more and more, flapping his wings so vigorously it hurt. Or was that why it hurt? Monty faltered as a wave of nausea twisted the world sideways. He felt . . . he felt . . .

Blood. He realized. He'd been hit.

Monty dared a glance back and caught sight of a deep gash down his left hind leg and a way-too-close manticore Defect inches from his tail. And he was smiling. Widely. Manticon faltered again. He knew the Defect had aimed for his wing, but hitting his leg might have been a better blow. The pain would take him out of the air, and the injury would prevent him from running.

He plummeted.

The wind smashed against his face as exhaustion flitted through his body, his wings hanging limp at his sides. He had lost a lot of blood. Little conscience was left for him to realize he was about to be a crushed heap on the ground. His face almost grazed the dirt when . . .

He was caught?

Monty felt long, thin talons wrap around his front legs and slide him on the ground. His mind was suddenly wide awake with adrenaline. Monty rolled over to find the griffin, eyes blaring, check him briskly and dart back into the sky. She took out the dragon by gripping its long horns and retching them to the side, snapping its neck in moments. Then she swung around and readied herself to take on the manticore. Monty almost cried at the hopelessness of that fight.

He was happily mistaken, though. The griffin was *insanely* fast, and ripped her elongated talons through his already-torn wings to widen the cuts before he so much as lifted a claw. He swung at her as she flung herself out of the attack, but just barely missed as he began to lose air. He fought as hard as he could to stay in the air, but his wings were too torn.

He was going down.

The griffin took the opportunity to dive into him, slice his throat, and push his body down hard into the ground. Just before she joined him as a squashed Morpher in the dirt, she barreled up and hovered above her kill with a predatory smile. The ground thundered when the massive manticore hit.

The griffin cocked her head toward Manticon. He cowered away, scared that she only saved him to take full credit for the catch. But she stayed where she was.

"Are you alright?" She asked him.

Monty tried to stand, but flopped back to the ground after putting weight on the leg. He shook his head. Knowing he couldn't move, the griffin landed next to him and circled Manticon until she found the brunt of his wound. She frowned.

"I should've taken him out earlier," she concluded, her talon lingering over his wound. Her eyes drifted over to Monty's, whose own were murky and terrified. She smiled, careful and pure. "The name is Quillis. I'm not with Parodem, I assure you. I'm only here to help."

"Why?" was all that Monty could muster. He was flat on his side with his bad leg up, and Quillis hovered right above it as if she were studying it.

The griffin dipped her head. "I'm old," she admitted. "I knew the old leader. He was rightful, he was honest, and he didn't send my children into battles that they'd surely lose." Tears bubbled in her eyes, and she looked away.

"The Allform raid?" Monty asked.

She nodded. "Young Morphers still. For griffins. Lost all three of my boys to the raid."

Monty gave her a sorrowful look. "I'm sorry."

She raised her head. "Don't worry, I'm making my mark. They'll be avenged. I wasn't expecting you to get wounded, so I don't have anything to help, but I'm willing to take you wherever you aim to go."

Monty sighed. "It's a long way from here, Quillis. I don't think they'd want you there either. You'd be better off leaving me to fend for myself. But thank you."

Quillis straightened, then smoothed back a tuft of feathers on her head. "I'm going to take you, kid. I don't know what you did, but I know that you don't support Parodem, so I'm going to help you regardless. Where are you going? And I suppose while we're on good terms, you have a name?"

"Manticon, but you can call me Monty," he said. "I'm going to the Allform kingdom."

"Oh," Quillis breathed, "that is a while from here. Alright then. I'll find something to bandage your leg and then we'll get moving, okay? And if you don't mind me asking, what in Motherstar's name are you hoping to find there?"

Monty quieted. He didn't know Quillis well, but she did save him. He owed her *something*. An explanation would have to do. "I'm hoping to find the last of the Allform royalty."

Quillis froze. "But they were killed."

"They were claimed dead," Monty corrected. "We only know that Parodem killed the queen. I'm looking for the princess."

"And what makes you believe the princess is still alive?"

Monty paused.

"I'm hoping that I'm the one who saved her. Before the raid, I told her. About the plan. I told her to run. Since that night, I hadn't heard from her. I hoped that I hadn't because she'd escaped," Manticon admitted. Quillis looked wide-eyed at him.

"You *knew* the Allform princess?" She asked, bewildered.

Monty smiled. "She was my best friend."

HALO AND PARODEM

It had been a long day for him. Parodem often got to spend all his time in his palace, but today he'd had other businesses to attend to. He'd had someone in his midst that he wasn't sure was against him until now. And he'd successfully rid of the infestation.

As he'd said, long day.

So Parodem skulked into his bedroom, flush with a massive canopy bed and glittering black furniture, and threw himself into his mattress. He was a leader, a savior to his kind. But most of all, at that moment, he was deathly exhausted.

When he had finally settled down, an odd creeping feeling crawled down his back.

Something was wrong.

Very wrong.

Parodem shuffled his covers back, pulling them off his tangled torso, and scanned his bedroom intently. As far as he could see, nothing off. But, he had caught assassins who had made their way into his castle before, and they never ended up making it out alive.

So Parodem was certain he could deal with another worthless Morpher assassin.

Parodem would've been *lucky* if an assassin was what had visited him, though.

"I'm honestly disgusted in myself for letting you sit there, gawking like the idiot you are, *alive*." A voice echoed around his room.

Parodem pulled himself off of the bed immediately, scanning the room once more. There wasn't a creature in sight, not even a presence that his heat-sensing could pick up. There was just the voice.

Then the sound of footsteps, but still no holder to them.

"The expression on your face, now - the pure terror - is something I could watch for a thousand years more." The voice laughed, but nothing was joyful about it. It was darker than a starless night. "You deserve every inch of that fear."

"Who are you?" Parodem growled, flitting his tiny wings and lifting himself into the air.

"A victim of your crimes," it answered.

Parodem turned his mouth in a cold-hearted smile. "None of my victims come out alive," he said proudly.

"I suppose that's true, but not a victim in that sense, you naive Defect. Your cruelty can run wild to those you don't even know still exist."

Defect. It called him a Defect.

"Show yourself, coward!" Parodem screamed into the air. The voice didn't say anything.

Instead, a brilliant flash of white light snapped at the far side of his room, and he sucked in a breath. Sitting in a glimmering throne of black obsidian sat a smug - but clearly furious - Allform. She was thin and young by Allform standards and hid under the protection of a white cloak, but screamed authority.

He'd killed an Allform before though.

He'd killed their *queen*.

What was one simple Allform going to do to him in his own domain?

Parodem started forward, charging straight at the still-dormant Allform.

The smirking Allform.

The Allform who clearly knew more than he did about their situation.

Before he could pull back, Parodem slammed into a sharp, translucent force field that only revealed itself after Parodem made contact with it.

Parodem collapsed to the ground, convulsing in pain that the stinging force field left shooting through his body.

The Allform snickered.

"For performing a raid on the Allform kingdom, you're extremely incompetent," the Allform purred, giving Parodem a smirk only worn by a devil. She stood up and bent at the hip, looked Parodem right in the eye, and growled, "Try again, and I won't hesitate to kill you. I'm not like the rest of my people - saps. I will kill you for everything you've done right here and now."

"Then why haven't you killed me yet?" Parodem challenged.

"I can't kill you just yet. Not at the moment. But if you push me to, I will, don't worry," she said with a bite in her tone, reaching up for her hood and pulling it off her head. When she dropped it, she bore a striking resemblance to someone that Parodem couldn't quite place.

"And why not?" He growled.

"Unlike you," she snapped, "*I* actually care about your people. I have motives."

Parodem clutched his stomach, flittering with sharp jabs of electricity, and stood to his full height. The Allform turned out to be much shorter than him, yet so much more powerful.

"Ah ah ah," the Allform sneered, stepping closer to Parodem and letting the forcefield follow her. "Either you back your sorry hind up, or I give you a world of pain you may never get out of."

Parodem reluctantly obeyed, maybe too well, and put nearly the whole room's distance in between them.

"How you've come across as such an imposing threat baffles me." She laughed again, her magenta eyes flashing with the threat of murder. "*You* are the coward here, Parodem."

"Who *are* you?" Parodem demanded. His demand was weak.

"Your downfall, Defect."

Parodem glared at the Allform, whose brow had twisted in pure disgust. "Then what is it that you have against me?"

The infuriated girl stalked forward, muscles tense and eyes black as night. "What do you think gives *you* the right to ask *me* that, murderer?" She stalked closer to him, and he pressed himself into the wall behind him out of fear. She saw his hesitation, his worry, and she smiled. "Keep doing that," she gestured to his quivering form, "and it just might save your life. It's empowering to see my mother's murderer cower to me."

Then it clicked.

The dead Allform princess.

Who clearly was not dead.

"There it is." She crossed her arms and cocked her head. "That realization. Give you any more fear, oh powerful leader of the Defects? That I'm *not* dead, and I have every little ounce of motivation to snap your neck and leave you for dead here and now for what you'v done? *Does it make you scared, Parodem?*"

It did. But he wasn't going to tell her that.

"Fool," she sneered, giving him another smirk. "I can hear you. I can hear your fear. You can't hide it."

Instead of stepping forward, the Allform princess turned her back to him and slithered back to the obsidian chair. Parodem was too terrified to move. And no matter how hard he tried to hide it, that overwhelming fear returned. This Allform wasn't anything like the rest of them.

She really would kill him.

And she wouldn't look back.

"You're dang right I wouldn't," the princess snapped from the throne. "You deserve to die. But your people don't deserve to suffer for your idiocy."

"I am *saving* my people. My plan will save them," Parodem argued.

"Your plan," the girl started, "is mass genocide. And you've already started it. So, Parodem," she grabbed her hood and slipped it back onto her head, "you'd better be ready. We're not warring with Castervile. We are warring with you."

Her force field flickered and shocked and vibrated until it vanished away, leaving her exposed to any of Parodem's attacks. That wasn't what worried him, though. What worried him most was the fact that it left *Parodem* exposed to *her*. She stalked forward once more, but instead of what Parodem first did - try and fight her - he shrunk back.

The white light that he knew he was going to grow to hate sparked around her, and she returned in his bedroom as a small, long blue dragon.

A dragon with ice slowly growing from its talons. Makeshift daggers. Deadly weapons.

"Heed my warning," she said, gripping an ice dagger as long as Parodem's forearm. "There's a lot more where this came from," and she reared up and impaled Parodem with the ice shard straight through the left side of his torso.

Parodem fell back, clutching the ice still jutting out of his side, and wondered why it didn't burn from his internal heat. But this Allform knew better, didn't she? She knew how to place a threat - about as well as Parodem did.

Or better.

Parodem howled in agony. His vision blurred, his heart sped up, and tiny daggers of pain shot up his side, arm, and chest in a spiral from the puncture. The Allform just stood and smiled. Watched him writhe in pain. Took pride in her revenge.

In the midst of the overwhelming pain, the girl left, but not before leaving one last warning.

"Oh, and I'd think it'd be nice if you kept this in mind. Your downfall? Her name is Halo."

Confession: Kirin and Canis Lu

Canis Lu wrung her hands and looked around. Today, she wouldn't tell *him* how she felt, but she'd tell his friend. His Dwellinghouse partner. Canis Lu's Sharehouse partner. It still made her nervous, no matter how hard she tried not to think of it. She'd promised herself that she'd tell Kirin about these feelings right after her training session with Omega, and more to her luck than not, Veado wasn't even home to eavesdrop.

So, tense as she could be, Canis Lu trudged into the Dwellinghouse yard with Kirin.

Also lucky for Canis Lu, Kirin was often blatantly oblivious. She likely wouldn't even notice if Canis Lu backed out of telling her the truth.

But she still would. She had to. It was already getting too pressing.

Though, maybe she shouldn't tell Kirin. Canis Lu hated the obvious looks of longing that Veado threw Kirin's way day after day after day. It seemed almost too true for her sake. So she stuck to her plan - tell Kirin. Chickening out was only a sign of weakness, even if Canis Lu would be the only one to know it.

She thought.

"What is up with you, Canis Lu? You've been awfully tense since we left Wolvendale." Kirin raised a brow. For Motherstar's sake, she wasn't as oblivious as Canis Lu had taken her for.

"Just . . . got something on my mind," Canis Lu answered with a fake smile. Maybe she'd actually believe Canis Lu. There might still be some obliviousness left.

Kirin gave Canis Lu a good stare and led her inside the Dwellinghouse. Before Canis Lu could back out - she was definitely feeling like doing so at that point - Kirin grabbed her arm and had her sit in a chair at their table. Then she sat down in front of Canis Lu and said, "What could possibly be on your mind already?"

That obliviousness left Kirin at the exact time Canis Lu didn't want it to.

Or maybe she just had a habit of thinking very little when it came to Kirin. After all, with the way Veado looked at her, Canis Lu couldn't help feeling like Kirin didn't deserve it.

Canis Lu pressed her ears down and refused to meet Kirin's eyes. She didn't care how obvious she made it. Kirin already had found out that *something* was wrong. Her tail curled around the chair like it was her anchor. Perhaps it was. Canis Lu didn't exactly enjoy not feeling snarky and confident, but this topic made her feel unnaturally and awkwardly weak.

"I suppose there is something I need to talk to you about," Canis Lu muttered.

"I gathered," Kirin said, waving her hand around to flick her hair back. She slouched back in her seat and crossed her arms, widening her eyes to ask for an answer.

For the love of Motherstar, when did she get so observant?

Then and again, she didn't really need to be. Canis Lu wasn't exactly being very tough about it.

"Soooo . . .?" Kirin pressed. "Problems with the wolves, questions about Forestlie, anything like that?" Well, maybe she was still stupid. That was, until Canis Lu blushed. "Oh." Kirin smirked. "A *boy*? Already?"

Canis Lu didn't want to answer, but she forced herself to nod. The hard part would be telling her who. After all, there wasn't a huge age gap between them. He was only about two moons older than her.

"Is it too far to ask who? Or are we not there yet?" It might have been too far, but that was why Canis Lu was here, right? She couldn't keep it bottled up any longer, and sadly Kirin was about the only one she could let it loose on. She thought.

Canis Lu smoothed back her hair and blurted out his name. "It's Veado," she breathed. She hated what she saw when she finally looked back up.

Kirin had gone completely still, so tense it looked like her skin would tear. Her pink eyes glinted a lifeless gleam and her shoulders shot up so high they nearly touched her ears.

That was what she was dreading.

While it looked like Veado had a crush on her, he didn't seem to be alone in that feeling. Kirin clearly had one on him too. Canis Lu's chances with him dwindled down to basically none. But would that stop the pounding in her heart? Most likely not. She'd probably have to hear the rejection from Veado himself to actually get rid of those feelings.

Canis Lu really, *really* didn't feel like walking into that one, though.

"Veado?" Kirin repeated, breathing life back into her eyes and letting her form go loose once more. "That's . . . oh." Kirin broke eye contact and glanced away, then turned back with something new sparking in her eyes. Something furious. Something dedicated.

It was something Canis Lu knew she wouldn't let out, but would bottle up just like her, and live in misery for that. But Canis Lu didn't really care.

Maybe, just maybe, it made her chances a little stronger.

As soon as the thought passed her mind, she cringed. It was cruel to think that, and yet she sat there with no remorse, totally believing every word her mind just uttered. Confidence bloomed back into her posture and she nodded, stiff and proud. It was awful, so very awful, but it didn't stop the hope from rising.

Maybe.

Just maybe.

"He's your Sharehouse partner," Kirin said, massaging her temples. "That's not weird to you?"

"He's only a couple moons older than me," Canis Lu answered. "It's not a massive difference, right?"

Kirin thought for a moment. "In time, no. But . . . you do realize we're supposed to be like parents to you, right? That's why *I'd* find it weird, but okay."

"I find you more like teachers." They were so close agewise that it didn't really bother her. They didn't seem like parents to her. They were closer to the title of "friends," though she wasn't sure she considered Kirin much in the first place.

Kirin nodded, but it was more than clear that she didn't accept it. Canis Lu had a feeling that would be her response.

Tension grew, and then Kirin barely whispered, "I like him too. Like . . . that." Then she pulled her fingers through her hair and slipped out of the chair. She paused before she hit the Dwellinghouse door, her hand lingering on the wood, and she said, "I can do my best to help train you, but because of this, I can't . . ." She trailed off but then straightened her back. "I'm not going to accept it or help you with it. I'm sorry, but I'm not ready to lose him."

And she pushed through the door, leaving Canis Lu in the dark.

She *knew* that would be how Kirin responded. Canis Lu knew calling it selfish immediately made her the selfish one, but her mind kept jumping to the accusation. Maybe it hadn't been smart to tell Kirin, because now the tension between them would be unbearable and deathly obvious.

But some awful part of Canis Lu took pride in Kirin's defeat. Some part of her grew stronger with a weakened competition.

Although, no matter how badly Canis Lu wanted to ignore it, she knew the truth.

If the choice were to be made, he'd choose Kirin.

That didn't stop Canis Lu from holding onto the glimpse of the feeling, though. She wouldn't let that go until she had to.

Until he told her himself.

Puma and Halo

Post-Storyline

The nights had been cold and unforgiving lately. Puma was used to those, though, as he used to live wherever he could in Skywake when he had no real home. It was only until that fateful night had the nights after been welcomingly cold and unforgiving. That night - that moment - Halo decided he was worth her while.

Well, if he was honest, he wasn't sure she *had* decided he was worth her while, but something had to have changed. He wasn't sure what moment changed him most though - the day they met (he remembered it to be *very* painful) or that moment after the war finally ended.

They'd gone in pairs that day, the six of them. Veado and Kirin had gone together, no argument there, and Halo had insisted on following Manticon for backup. That left Puma stranded with the tag-along Allform, roaming the hidden labyrinths of Parodem's creepy palace. He'd only decided on coming because . . . well, because Halo was there. He didn't know why, not at the time, but he couldn't help being drawn to the girl who might've nearly killed him the first day they met. He knew now, though. After spending day after day living luxuriously in her castle, with her, he learned he could never get enough of the Allform princess.

He loved her.

It was a realization that dawned on him the moment Halo brought him home with her.

He really loved her, even her jumpier-than-normal self.

Sadly, he didn't know what happened with Halo and Monty when they went into Parodem's palace, but whatever it was had been haunting Halo ever since Manticon was claimed leader of Casterville. She'd been paranoid, lost, and even anxious ever since the palace raid. Puma only wished she'd tell him why. But knowing poor Halo, she wouldn't. She'd hold it in to the very moment it shattered her and only then would she tell him, but only half of it. She'd never tell it all to him. That hurt Puma more than he wanted to admit.

Puma had been keen to roam Halo's palace at night. He didn't know why, exactly, that he did it, but he guessed maybe it just helped him get acquainted with Allform life. After all, it was *so* much more advanced than Morpher life was. Morphers relied on the environment and Motherstar's gracious gifts, while Allforms . . . they made their own gifts, created their own pristine world. It was fascinating.

And a little harsh, sadly.

Most of the Allforms didn't enjoy a simple Morpher like himself dwindling among them, or better yet, living in the Allform palace with their princess. Halo had actually protected Puma more than she wanted him to know, but it hadn't stopped the angry, disapproving eyes.

He wasn't wanted here. He couldn't blame them for that either.

Puma flicked his ears, eyes straying down the long white corridor. Allforms liked white for its "purity" and bathed their entire city and palace in the color. Puma didn't mind it much, honestly. At the end of the hallway, a long, elegant window stretched across the wall, dousing the hallway in brilliant moonlight. Puma breathed a scarce breath. The palace was always beautiful, unnervingly so, but his breath caught for a different reason.

The moon drew a thin beam of light to a single door, a door that Puma's heart sped up at the sight of.

The Allform princess's.

The door was cracked open, and a soft noise floated through the hallway from her room.

Puma sucked in another shaky breath. He couldn't be hearing that, right?

The noise sounded all too much like she was *crying*.

Puma skulked forward to the door, slowly wrapping his fingers around the wood and tenderly pushing it open. Halo was doubled over on her bed, head in hands, sobbing as softly as she could. Her gorgeous white hair was matted and wet from tears, and her night garments, normally perfect, were soaked and crumpled. Puma nearly gasped, but his mind wasn't as silent as his body.

Halo's head snapped up. She scowled, something more familiar to Puma, and immediately reached up to wipe the lingering tears on her face. Her brows furrowed in a deep but embarrassed frown.

"Puma," she sputtered as formally as she could. A forced glare masked her expression. "What are you doing up at this hour?"

Puma pressed the door all the way open and hovered in the doorway. "I heard crying." Halo's firm eyes softened, and her tears seemed to be forcing their way back out.

Halo tore her gaze away from him and faced the window behind her. "I'm fine," she lied. She sniffled and reached for her hair to try and fix it, but Puma was next to her in moments sporting a soft smile. He reached for her hand to stop her from messing with her hair, but she jumped back and fell into the pillow behind her. She wouldn't look at him.

Puma sat on the foot of the bed as far as he felt comfortable for her. Halo threw her legs off the side of the bed and sat parallel to him, but quickly drew her legs up to her head in embarrassment. Puma had no idea what to say other than "What's wrong?"

It took him all the courage in the world to approach her, but so much more to watch the powerful heir shrivel into herself and weep without knowing how in the slightest to help her. Halo wiped a stray tear and sniffled again, but finally looked at Puma. His heart nearly vibrated out of his chest.

"I messed up - bad, Puma, really bad. I-" Halo broke into another sob. "I don't want to be the reason he dies like I was for my mother." She choked. Puma held in the shock that pounded against his brain - *she told him*.

"I-"

Halo shook her head. "You don't know what happened that day. I could be the reason all of Castervile caves in - *my* actions. My greed."

Puma's eyes widened. "You killed him," he realized. Halo nodded weakly. He knew there was supposed to be some detrimental reason that only Monty could be the one to kill Parodem, but Puma also knew that if any harm came to him, Halo wouldn't have been able to hold back. And it sounded like she didn't.

After Parodem had been confirmed dead, that was when Puma took off. He never had any reason to think that anyone other than Manticon had killed the corrupt Castervillain leader, so he didn't even try to think otherwise. It must've been tearing Halo apart from inside out ever since she did it. She must've thought she'd doomed Monty should any creature find out. Puma's face fell into a concerned frown.

"It's not your fault, Halo," he said simply. "Maybe I don't know what happened, but I do know that Manticon is alive today because of you. Castervile is working on reforming because of you. Halo, they're no longer addressed as *villains* because of what you did. Even if it didn't follow tradition, it gave a whole kingdom another name, another chance. And Monty will be okay, don't worry."

Halo's eyes almost sparkled as she watched Puma, but he couldn't tell if it was from the tears or admiration. Probably the tears. Puma wasn't sure he believed that Halo could look at him with admiration. It still made him want to hug her, no matter how much the secluded Allform would resist. He knew better, though.

Her eyes dulled. "But-"

"No," Puma said quickly. She was going to kill him for this later. "No 'buts.' You saved the world, Halo. You saved the world and pinned it on someone else. You're a silent hero, and those are the best kind. You did everything you could. You saved him, not doomed him."

Halo's eyes found Puma's again, and he couldn't help a shudder. *She's beautiful, even when she doesn't mean to be.* Puma shoved the thought out of his head as quickly as he could, though, annoyed at Halo's ability to read minds. A small smile tugged at her lips - she heard him.

The princess looked away, watching the floor, and ran one hand through her hair. It was a tangled mess that didn't cooperate in the slightest when she tried to brush through it, but she paid no mind. "Maybe-" Halo began suddenly. She paused, shook her head, and let out a heavy sigh. "Maybe it's not impossible, you and I."

Puma started back, eyes wide. He'd been in love with the princess since he met her and because of her awful mindreading, she'd known. She'd never openly turned him down, but her knowing about his little crush was enough to hint at it. Although, she'd never decided to bring up his feelings to him before either, so this was different.

It all came crashing back - the moment his life changed for the better. He'd run from the Castervillain palace, from the Allform he was paired with. He ran hoping to find a better life. He wanted to go with Halo, he really did, but he wasn't sure she'd let him. He ran through the deserted Castervillain streets, through the Defect Morphers who were drafted into this war. No one was there to see him escape. Halo wouldn't know where he was and probably wouldn't give him another thought. As he started to run past the boundaries of Castervile, straight into the Lost Lands, he'd heard it.

The wingbeats.

He'd thought someone was coming for him, but he found himself watching the Allforms retreat back home.

He would've been hidden if it weren't for the princess, who caught just a sliver of his mind and saw him hiding down below her and her people. She went down to meet him. He'd never planned for that to happen. In fact, he froze almost as soon as she laid eyes on him, but she didn't look like her cold, normal self. She looked at him with pity.

"Puma," she had breathed, scanning him up and down. "I thought you were still in the palace."

Puma didn't answer, just did his best to look away from her. It was difficult, though, as the Allform princess was nothing short of breathtaking. She popped a brow. Puma sighed.

"I- sorry," he had said, his head hanging. "I couldn't stay there. I wouldn't be accepted. I needed to find a home before I could . . . settle, I guess."

Halo cocked her head with a frown. She had known he was lying. *I want to go with you, Halo*, he thought silently to himself.

"Ask me," she said simply.

Puma was at a loss for words. "What? I- uhm . . ."

"Ask me, Puma. Do it."

He let out a strained breath. "I want . . . Halo, I want to go with you to the Allform kingdom. I- please," he choked.

For the longest time, he thought it was a joke. A cruel, awful moment where she would simply say, "you can't" and move on. Leave. Abandon him there. But she looked at him so kindly, so un-Halo-like, and gave him a small genuine smile. A meaningful smile. Something Puma could never forget, not ever from that day forward. The moment Halo looked at him - maybe even saw him - differently.

And she took him. No words were passed between them from then until they got to the Allform kingdom, but none were needed. And, quite honestly, Puma may not have been able to form any words after that, let alone a full sentence. He was still in a little bit of disbelief.

Now, here he was, sitting in front of the same beautiful secluded girl who gave him a reason for life, saying that there was a chance. A possibility. Her tears had dried, and although her hair was still a mess and her clothes were still crumpled, she couldn't look more perfect. More . . .

A thought crossed his head, a thought he wished he hadn't had right in front of her.

He wanted to kiss her.

Halo flinched as his thought met her mind. Puma's heart plummeted.

She started to turn away, head bowed, and Puma took it as his cue to leave. He stood up, glanced at Halo, and began to walk away, but Halo snatched his wrist before he could go far. He didn't have enough time to realize what was happening. In fact, he never would've expected it. He was ready to accept defeat. It hurt, but he knew the princess had more than him on her mind. He could - he *would* accept it, just for her.

But he never would have believed in that moment that it was *Halo* who had kissed *him*.